E. NESBIT'S TALES OF TERROR

Terrifying stories

of suspense,

mystery and horror

from a mistress

of the macabre

E. NESBIT'S TALES OF TERROR

Edited by Hugh Lamb

Illustrated by Sue Stitt

A Magnet Book

First published 1983 by Methuen London Ltd
This Magnet edition published 1985 by Methuen London Ltd
11 New Fetter Lane, London EC4P 4EE
This anthology copyright © 1983 Hugh Lamb
Illustrations copyright © 1983 Sue Stitt
Reproduced, printed and bound in Great Britain by
Hazell Watson & Viney Limited,
Aylesbury, Bucks

ISBN 0 416 51830 3

Contents

Foreword

E. Nesbit today is best known for her famous children's books. These tell enchanting stories of magic and adventure. Films of *The Phoenix and the Carpet*, *The Treasure Seekers*, *The Enchanted Castle* and *The Railway Children* have recently delighted a new generation of children.

But Edith Nesbit started her literary life in a very different genre. She wrote ghost stories. Many of these have never been reprinted since they first appeared in the 1880s and have been lost to readers for generations. Here is a selection of them. They show her to have been as much a mistress of the macabre as she was of adventure, magic and humour.

*

Born in London in 1858, Edith Nesbit was the daughter of a teacher and scientist. She was educated in England and on the continent where the family spent eight years after her father's death. She is said to have lived in at least two haunted houses in her childhood!

She started writing early in life, and was forced to take it seriously when her husband's business partner absconded with the capital. In a desperate effort to earn money, she sent stories to magazines. They were accepted and she found herself much in demand for her work. This was the period when she wrote most of her tales of terror. They appeared first in magazines and were later collected into volumes of stories.

Edith Nesbit was a very successful writer for many years. Her career had declined by 1910 but she enjoyed a revival toward the end of her life, and wrote some more ghost stories then. She died in 1924.

Her ghost stories and tales of terror have their roots in childhood fears firmly implanted in the author's memory.

In 1896, she described a childhood visit to see the mummified corpses in the church of Saint Michel, Bordeaux. They were 'the crowning horror of my childish life ... it is to them, I think, more than to any other thing that I owe nights and nights of anguish and horror, long years of bitterest fear and dread'. But she obviously enjoyed as good a fright as anyone: her biographer, Doris Langley Moore, records that Edith 'would sit up at night writing tales of violence and death until she was afraid to go to bed ... she would read books and see sights which, as she was fully aware beforehand, were certain to upset her nerves'.

There is no doubt that she wrote her stories to get rid of her own fears (though one wonders how successful this therapy was). The peculiar type of horror in *Man-size in Marble*, for instance, can be traced back to those Bordeaux mummies. Apparently Edith had a relative who had actually been placed in his coffin, presumed dead, before it was noticed he was breathing; this induced a terrible dread in her of being buried alive, and *The Five Senses* sees her giving full rein to this terror.

Readers today should be pleasantly surprised at the wide range of Edith Nesbit's tales of terror. She rings the changes between straightforward ghost story (as in *John Charrington's Wedding*), creepy tale (*The Violet Car*), and early science fiction (*The Three Drugs*) very successfully, and is not afraid of downright horror (*In The Dark*).

Those familiar with Edith Nesbit from her children's books, and those who have never yet read anything by her, are in for a treat. I hope her stories find the wide audience they deserve.

HUGH LAMB
Sutton, Surrey

For Richard and Andrew
who like a good fright

IN THE DARK

It may have been a form of madness. Or it may be that he really was what is called haunted. Or it may – though I don't pretend to understand how – have been the development, through intense suffering, of a sixth sense in a very nervous, highly-strung nature. Something certainly led him where They were. And to him They were all one.

He told me the first part of the story, and the last part of it I saw with my own eyes.

I

Haldane and I were friends even in our school-days. What first brought us together was our common hatred of Visger, who came from our part of the country. His people knew our people at home, so he was put on to us when he came. He was the most intolerable person, boy and man, that I have ever known. He would not tell a lie. And that was all right. But he didn't stop at that. If he were asked whether any other chap had done anything – been out of bounds, or up to any sort of lark – he would always say, 'I don't know, sir, but I believe so.' He never did know – we took care of that. But what he believed was always right. I remember Haldane twisting his arm to say how he knew about that cherry-tree business, and he only said, 'I don't know – I just feel sure. And I was right, you see.' What can you do with a boy like that?

We grew up to be men. At least Haldane and I did. Visger grew up to be a prig. He was a vegetarian and a teetotaler, and an all-wooler and a Christian Scientist, and all the things that prigs are – but he wasn't a common prig. He knew all sorts of things that he oughtn't to have known, that he *couldn't* have known in any ordinary decent way. It wasn't that he found things out. He just knew them. Once, when I was very unhappy, he came into my rooms – we were all in our last year at Oxford – and talked about things I hardly knew myself. That was really why I went to India that winter. It was bad enough to be unhappy, without having that beast knowing all about it.

I was away over a year. Coming back, I thought a lot about how jolly it would be to see old Haldane again. If I thought about Visger at all, I wished he was dead. But I didn't think about him much.

I did want to see Haldane. He was always such a jolly chap – gay, and kindly, and simple, honourable, upright, and full of practical sympathies. I longed to see him, to see the smile in his jolly blue eyes, looking out from the net of wrinkles that laughing had made round them, to hear his jolly laugh, and feel the good grip of his big hand. I went straight from the docks to his chambers in Gray's Inn, and I found him cold, pale, anaemic, with dull eyes and a limp hand, and pale lips that smiled without mirth, and uttered a welcome without gladness.

He was surrounded by a litter of disordered furniture and personal effects half packed. Some big boxes stood corded, and there were cases of books, filled and waiting for the enclosing boards to be nailed on.

'Yes, I'm moving,' he said. 'I can't stand these rooms. There's something rum about them – something devilish rum. I clear out tomorrow.'

The autumn dusk was filling the corners with shadows. 'You got the furs,' I said, just for something to say, for I saw the big case that held them lying corded among the others.

'Furs?' he said. 'Oh yes. Thanks awfully. Yes. I forgot about the furs.' He laughed, out of politeness, I suppose, for there was no joke about the furs. They were many and fine – the best I could get for money, and I had seen them packed and sent off when my heart was very sore. He stood looking at me, and saying nothing.

'Come out and have a bit of dinner,' I said as cheerfully as I could.

'Too busy,' he answered, after the slightest possible pause and a glance round the room – 'look here – I'm awfully glad to see you – If you'd just slip over and order in dinner – I'd go myself – only – Well, you see how it is.'

I went. And when I came back, he had cleared a space near the fire, and moved his big gate-table into it. We dined there by candle light. I tried to be amusing. He, I am sure, tried to be amused. We did not succeed, either of us. And his haggard eyes watched me all the time, save in those fleeting moments when, without turning his head, he glanced back over his shoulder into the shadows that crowded round the little lighted place where we sat.

When we had dined and the man had come and taken away the dishes, I looked at Haldane very steadily, so that he stopped in a pointless anecdote, and looked interrogation at me.

'Well?' I said.

'You're not listening,' he said petulantly. 'What's the matter?'

'That's what you'd better tell me,' I said.

He was silent, gave one of those furtive glances at the shadows, and stooped to stir the fire to – I knew it – a blaze that must light every corner of the room.

'You're all to pieces,' I said cheerfully. 'What have you been up to? Wine? Cards? Speculation? A woman? If you won't tell me, you'll have to tell your doctor. Why, my dear chap, you're a wreck.'

'You're a comfortable friend to have about the place,' he said, and smiled a mechanical smile not at all pleasant to see.

'I'm the friend you want, I think,' said I. 'Do you suppose I'm blind? Something's gone wrong and you've taken to something. Morphia, perhaps? And you've brooded over the thing till you've lost all sense of proportion. Out with it, old chap. I bet you a dollar it's not so bad as you think it.'

'If I could tell you – or tell anyone,' he said slowly, 'it wouldn't be so bad as it is. If I could tell anyone, I'd tell you. And even as it is, I've told you more than I've told anyone else.'

I could get nothing more out of him. But he pressed me to stay – would have given me his bed and made himself a shake-down, he said. But I had engaged my room at the Victoria, and I was expecting letters. So I left him, quite late – and he stood on the stairs, holding a candle over the bannisters to light me down.

When I went back next morning, he was gone. Men were moving his furniture into a big van with Somebody's Pantechnicon painted on it in big letters.

He had left no address with the porter, and had driven off in a hansom with two portmanteaux – to Waterloo, the porter thought.

Well, a man has a right to the monopoly of his own troubles, if he chooses to have it. And I had troubles of my own that kept me busy.

II

It was more than a year later that I saw Haldane again. I had got rooms in the Albany by this time, and he turned up there one morning, very early indeed – before breakfast in fact. And if he looked ghastly before, he now looked almost ghostly. His face looked as though it had worn thin, like an oyster shell that has for years been cast up twice a day by the sea on a shore all pebbly. His hands were thin as birds' claws, and they trembled like caught butterflies.

I welcomed him with enthusiastic cordiality and pressed breakfast on him. This time, I decided, I would ask no questions. For I saw that none were needed. He would tell me. He intended to tell me. He had come here to tell me, and for nothing else.

I lit the spirit lamp, I made coffee and small talk for him, and I ate and drank, and waited for him to begin. And it was like this that he began:

'I am going,' he said, 'to kill myself – oh, don't be alarmed,' – I suppose I had said or looked something – 'I shan't do it here, or now. I shall do it when I have to – when I can't bear it any longer. And I want someone to know why. I don't want to feel that I'm the only living creature who does know. And I can trust you, can't I?'

I murmured something reassuring.

'I should like you, if you don't mind, to give me your word, that you won't tell a soul what I'm going to tell you, as long as I'm alive. Afterwards ... you can tell whom you please.'

I gave him my word.

He sat silent looking at the fire. Then he shrugged his shoulders.

'It's extraordinary how difficult it is to say it,' he said, and smiled. 'The fact is – you know that beast, George Visger.'

'Yes,' I said. 'I haven't seen him since I came back. Someone told me he'd gone to some island or other to preach vegetarianism to the cannibals. Anyhow, he's out of the way, bad luck to him.'

'Yes,' said Haldane, 'he's out of the way. But he's not preaching anything. In point of fact, he's dead.'

'Dead?' was all I could think of to say.

'Yes,' said he; 'it's not generally known, but he is.'

'What did he die of?' I asked, not that I cared. The bare fact was good enough for me.

'You know what an interfering chap he always was. Always knew everything. Heart to heart talks – and have everything open and above board. Well, he interfered between me and someone else – told her a pack of lies.'

'Lies?'

'Well, the *things* were true, but he made lies of them the way he told them – *you* know.' I did. I nodded. 'And she

threw me over. And she died. And we weren't even friends.
And I couldn't see her – before – I couldn't even ... Oh,
my God ... But I went to the funeral. He was there.
They'd asked *him*. And then I came back to my rooms.
And I was sitting there, thinking. And he came up.'

'He would do. It's just what he would do. The beast! I
hope you kicked him out.'

'No, I didn't. I listened to what he'd got to say. He came
to say, No doubt it was all for the best. And he hadn't
known the things he told her. He'd only guessed. He'd
guessed right, damn him. What right had he to guess
right? And he said it was all for the best, because, besides
that, there was madness in my family. He'd found that out
too –'

'And is there?'

'If there is, I didn't know it. And that was why it was all
for the best. So then I said, "There wasn't any madness in
my family before, but there is now," and I got hold of his
throat. I am not sure whether I meant to kill him; I ought
to have meant to kill him. Anyhow, I did kill him. What
did you say?'

I had said nothing. It is not easy to think at once of the
tactful and suitable thing to say, when your oldest friend
tells you that he is a murderer.

'When I could get my hands out of his throat, – it was
as difficult as it is to drop the handles of a galvanic battery
– he fell in a lump on the hearth-rug. And I saw what I'd
done. How is it that murderers ever get found out?'

'They're careless, I suppose,' I found myself saying,
'they lose their nerve.'

'I didn't,' he said. 'I never was calmer. I sat down in the
big chair and looked at him, and thought it all out. He
was just off to that island – I knew that. He'd said good-
bye to everyone. He'd told me that. There was no blood to
get rid of – or only just a touch at the corner of his slack
mouth. He wasn't going to travel in his own name because
of interviewers. Mr Somebody Something's luggage would

be unclaimed and his cabin empty. No one would guess that Mr Somebody Something was Sir George Visger, F.R.S. It was all as plain as plain. There was nothing to get rid of, but the man. No weapon, no blood – and I got rid of him all right.'

'How?'

He smiled cunningly.

'No, no,' he said; 'that's where I draw the line. It's not that I doubt your word, but if you talked in your sleep, or had a fever or anything. No, No. As long as you don't know where the body is, don't you see, I'm all right. Even if you could prove that I've said all this – which you can't – it's only the wanderings of my poor unhinged brain. See?'

I saw. And I was sorry for him. And I did not believe that he had killed Visger. He was not the sort of man who kills people. So I said:

'Yes, old chap, I see. Now look here. Let's go away together, you and I – travel a bit and see the world, and forget all about that beastly chap.'

His eyes lighted up at that.

'Why,' he said, 'you understand. You don't hate me and shrink from me. I wish I'd told you before – you know – when you came and I was packing all my sticks. But it's too late now.'

'Too late? Not a bit of it,' I said. 'Come, we'll pack our traps and be off tonight – out into the unknown, don't you know.'

'That's where *I'm* going,' he said. 'You wait. When you've heard what's been happening to me, you won't be so keen to go travelling about with me.'

'But you've told me what's been happening to you,' I said, and the more I thought about what he had told me, the less I believed it.

'No,' he said, slowly, 'no – I've told you what happened to *him*. What happened to me is quite different. Did I tell you what his last words were? Just when I was coming at

him. Before I'd got his throat, you know. He said, "Look
out. You'll never be able to get rid of the body. Besides,
anger's sinful." You know that way he had, like a tract on
its hind legs. So afterwards I got thinking of that. But I
didn't think of it for a year. Because I did get rid of his
body all right. And then I was sitting in that comfortable
chair, and I thought, "Hullo, it must be about a year now,
since that –" and I pulled out my pocket-book and went
to the window to look at a little almanack I carry about –
it was getting dusk – and sure enough it was a year, to the
day. And then I remembered what he'd said. And I said
to myself, "Not much trouble about getting rid of *your*
body, you brute." And then I looked at the hearth-rug
and – Ah!' – he screamed suddenly and very loud – 'I can't
tell you – no, I can't.'

My man opened the door – he wore a smooth face over
his wriggling curiosity. 'Did you call, sir?'

'Yes,' I lied. 'I want you to take a note to the bank, and
wait for an answer.'

When he was got rid of, Haldane said: 'Where was
I? –'

'You were just telling me what happened after you
looked at the almanack. What was it?'

'Nothing much,' he said, laughing softly, 'oh, nothing
much – only that I glanced at the hearthrug – and there
he was – the man I'd killed a year before. Don't try to
explain, or I shall lose my temper. The door was shut. The
windows were shut. He hadn't been there a minute before.
And he was there then. That's all.'

Hallucination was one of the words I stumbled among.

'Exactly what I thought,' he said triumphantly, 'but –
I touched it. It was quite real. Heavy, you know, and
harder than live people are somehow, to the touch – more
like a stone thing covered with kid the hands were, and
the arms like a marble statue in a blue serge suit. Don't
you hate men who wear blue serge suits?'

'There are hallucinations of touch too,' I found myself

saying.

'Exactly what I thought,' said Haldane more triumphant than ever, 'but there are limits, you know – limits. So then I thought someone had got him out – the real him – and stuck him there to frighten me, while my back was turned, and I went to the place where I'd hidden him, and he was there – ah! – just as I'd left him. Only ... it was a year ago. There are two of him there now.'

'My dear chap,' I said, 'this is simply comic.'

'Yes,' he said, 'it is amusing. I find it so myself. Especially in the night when I wake up and think of it. I hope I shan't die in the dark, Winston: That's one of the reasons why I think I shall have to kill myself. I could be sure then of not dying in the dark.'

'Is *that* all?' I asked, feeling sure that it must be.

'No,' said Haldane at once. 'That's *not* all. He's come back to me again. In a railway carriage it was. I'd been asleep. When I woke up, there he was lying on the seat opposite me. Looking just the same. I pitched him out on the line in Red Hill Tunnel. And if I see him again, I'm going out myself. I can't stand it. It's too much. I'd sooner go. Whatever the next world's like, there aren't things in it like that. We leave them here, in graves and boxes and ... You think I'm mad. But I'm not. You can't help me – no one can help me. He *knew*, you see. He said I shouldn't be able to get rid of the body. And I can't get rid of it. I can't. I can't. He knew. He always did know things that he *couldn't* know. But I'll cut his game short. After all, I've got the ace of trumps, and I play it on his next trick. I give you my word of honour, Winston, that I'm not mad.'

'My dear old man,' I said, 'I don't think you're mad. But I do think your nerves are very much upset. Mine are a bit, too. Do you know why I went to India? It was because of you and her. I couldn't stay and see it, though I wished for your happiness and all that; you know I did. And when I came back, she ... and you ... Let's see it out together,' I said. 'You won't keep fancying things if you've got me to talk to. And I always said you weren't half a bad old duffer.'

'She liked you,' he said.

'Oh, yes,' I said, 'she liked me.'

III

That was how we came to go abroad together. I was full of hope for him. He'd always been such a splendid chap – so sane and strong. I couldn't believe that he was gone mad, gone for ever, I mean, so that he'd never come right again. Perhaps my own trouble made it easy for me to see things not quite straight. Anyway, I took him away to recover his mind's health, exactly as I should have taken him away to get strong after a fever. And the madness seemed to pass away, and in a month or two we were perfectly jolly, and I thought I had cured him. And I was very glad because of that old friendship of ours, and because she had loved him and liked me.

We never spoke of Visger. I thought he had forgotten all about him. I thought I understood how his mind, over-strained by sorrow and anger, had fixed on the man he hated, and woven a nightmare web of horror round that detestable personality. And I had got the whip hand of my own trouble. And we were as jolly as sandboys together all those months.

And we came to Bruges at last in our travels, and Bruges was very full, because of the Exhibition. We could only get one room and one bed. So we tossed for the bed, and the one who lost the toss was to make the best of the night in the arm-chair. And the bed-clothes we were to share equitably.

We spent the evening at a *café chantant* and finished at a beer hall, and it was late and sleepy when we got back to the Grande Vigne. I took our key from its nail in the concierge's room, and we went up. We talked awhile, I remember, of the town, and the belfry, and the Venetian aspect of the canals by moonlight, and then Haldane got into bed, and I made a chrysalis of myself with my share of the blankets and fitted the tight roll into the armchair. I was not at all comfortable, but I was compensatingly tired, and I was nearly asleep when Haldane roused me up to tell me about his will.

'I've left everything to you, old man,' he said. 'I know I can trust you to see to everything.'

'Quite so,' said I, 'and if you don't mind, we'll talk about it in the morning.'

He tried to go on about it, and about what a friend I'd been, and all that, but I shut him up and told him to go to sleep. But no. He wasn't comfortable, he said. And he'd got a thirst like a lime kiln. And he'd noticed that there was no water-bottle in the room. 'And the water in the jug's like pale soup,' he said.

'Oh, all right,' said I. 'Light your candle and go and get some water, then, in Heaven's name, and let me get to sleep.'

But he said, 'No – you light it. I don't want to get out of bed in the dark. I might – I might step on something, mightn't I – or walk into something that wasn't there when I got into bed.'

'Rot,' I said, 'walk into your grandmother.' But I lit the candle all the same. He sat up in bed and looked at me – very pale – with his hair all tumbled from the pillow, and his eyes blinking and shining.

'That's better,' he said. And then, 'I say – look here. Oh – yes – I see. It's all right. Queer how they mark the sheets here. Blest if I didn't think it was blood, just for the minute.'

The sheet was marked, not at the corner, as sheets are marked at home, but right in the middle where it turns down, with big, red, cross-stitching.

'Yes, I see,' I said, 'it is a queer place to mark it.'

'It's queer letters to have on it,' he said. 'G. V.'

'Grande Vigne,' I said, 'What letters do you expect them to mark things with? Hurry up.'

'You come too,' he said. 'Yes, it does stand for Grande Vigne, of course. I wish you'd come down too, Winston.'

'I'll *go* down,' I said and turned with the candle in my hand.

He was out of bed and close to me in a flash. 'No,' said he, 'I don't want to stay alone in the dark.'

He said it just as a frightened child might have done.

'All right then, come along,' I said. And we went. I tried to make some joke, I remember, about the length of his hair, and the cut of his pyjamas – but I was sick with disappointment. For it was almost quite plain to me, even then, that all my time and trouble had been thrown away, and that he wasn't cured after all. We went down as quietly as we could, and got a carafe of water from the long bare dining table in the salle-à-manger. He got hold of my arm at first, and then he got the candle away from me, and went very slowly, shading the light with his hand, and looking very carefully all about, as though he expected to see something that he wanted very desperately not to see. And of course, I knew what that something was. I didn't like the way he was going on. I can't at all express how deeply I didn't like it. And he looked over his shoulder every now and then, just as he did that first evening after I came back from India.

The thing got on my nerves so that I could hardly find the way back to our room. And when we got there, I give you my word, I more than half expected to see what *he* had expected to see – that, or something like that, on the hearth-rug. But of course there was nothing.

I blew out the light and tightened my blankets round me – I'd been trailing them after me in our expedition. And I was settled in my chair when Haldane spoke.

'You've got all the blankets,' he said.

'No, I haven't,' said I, 'only what I've always had.'

'I can't find mine then,' he said, and I could hear his teeth chattering. 'And I'm cold. I'm ... For God's sake, light the candle. Light it. Light it. Something horrible ...'

And I couldn't find the matches.

'Light the candle, light the candle,' he said, and his voice broke, as a boy's does sometimes in chapel. 'If you don't he'll come to me. It is so easy to come at anyone in the dark. Oh Winston, light the candle, for the love of God! I can't die in the dark.'

'I am lighting it,' I said savagely, and I was feeling for the matches on the marble-topped chest of drawers, on the mantelpiece – everywhere but on the round centre table where I'd put them. 'You're not going to die. Don't be a fool,' I said. 'It's all right. I'll get a light in a second.'

He said, 'It's cold. It's cold. It's cold,' like that, three times. And then he screamed aloud, like a woman – like a child – like a hare when the dogs have got it. I had heard him scream like that once before.

'What is it?' I cried, hardly less loud. 'For God's sake, hold your noise. What is it?'

There was an empty silence. Then, very slowly:

'It's Visger,' he said. And he spoke thickly, as through some stifling veil.

'Nonsense. Where?' I asked, and my hand closed on the matches as he spoke.

'Here,' he screamed sharply, as though he had torn the veil away, 'here, beside me. In the bed.'

I got the candle alight. I got across to him.

He was crushed in a heap at the edge of the bed. Stretched on the bed beyond him was a dead man, white and very cold.

Haldane had died in the dark.

It was all so simple.

We had come to the wrong room. The man the room

belonged to was there, on the bed he had engaged and paid for before he died of heart disease, earlier in the day. A French *commis-voyageur* representing soap and perfumery; his name, Felix Leblanc.

Later, in England, I made cautious enquiries. The body of a man had been found in the Red Hill tunnel – a haberdasher man named Simmons, who had drunk spirits of salts, owing to the depression of trade. The bottle was clutched in his dead hand.

For reasons that I had, I took care to have a police inspector with me when I opened the boxes that came to me by Haldane's will. One of them was the big box, metal-lined, in which I had sent him the skins from India – for a wedding present, God help us all!

It was closely soldered.

Inside were the skins of beasts? No. The bodies of two men. One was identified, after some trouble, as that of a hawker of pens in city offices – subject to fits. He had died in one, it seemed. The other body was Visger's, right enough.

Explain it as you like. I offered you, if you remember, a choice of explanations before I began the story. I have not yet found the explanation that can satisfy me.

MAN-SIZE IN MARBLE

Although every word of this tale is true, I do not expect people to believe it. Nowadays a 'rational explanation' is required before belief is possible. Let me, at once, offer the 'rational explanation' which finds most favour among those who have heard the tale of my life's tragedy. It is held that we were 'under a delusion', she and I, on that 31st of October; and that this supposition places the whole matter on a satisfactory and believable basis. The reader can judge, when he, too, has heard my story, how far this is an 'explanation', and in what sense it is 'rational'. There were three who took part in this; Laura and I and another man. The other man lives still, and can speak to the truth of the least credible part of my story.

I never knew in my life what it was to have as much money as would supply the most ordinary needs of life – good colours, canvasses, brushes, books and cab-fares – and when we were married, we knew quite well that we should only be able to live at all by 'strict punctuality and attention to business'. I used to paint in those days, and Laura used to write, and we felt sure we could keep the pot at least simmering. Living in London was out of the question, so we went to look for a cottage in the country, which should be at once sanitary and picturesque. So rarely do these two qualities meet in one cottage that our search was for some time quite fruitless. We tried advertisements, but most of the desirable rural residences which we did look at, proved to be lacking in both essentials, and when a cottage chanced to have drains, it always had stucco as well and was shaped like a tea-caddy. And if we found a vine or a rose-covered porch, corruption invariably lurked within. Our minds got so befogged by the eloquence of house-agents, and the rival disadvantages of the fever-traps and outrages to beauty which we had seen and scorned, that I very much doubt whether either of us, on our wedding morning, knew the difference between a house and a haystack. But when we got away from friends and house-agents on our honeymoon, our wits grew clear again, and we knew a pretty cottage when at last we saw one. It was at Brenzett – a little village set on a hill, over against the southern marshes. We had gone there from the little fishing village, where we were staying, to see the church, and two fields from the church we found this cottage. It stood quite by itself about two miles from Brenzett village. It was a low building with rooms sticking out in unexpected places. There was a bit of stonework – ivy-covered and moss-grown, just two old rooms, all that was left of a big house that once stood there – and round this stonework the house had grown up. Stripped of its roses and jasmine, it would have been hideous. As it stood it was charming, and after a brief examination, enthusiasm usurped the place of discretion and we took it. It was absurdly cheap. The rest of our honeymoon we spent in grubbing about in second-hand shops in Ashford, picking up bits of old oak and Chippendale chairs for our furnishing. We wound up with a run up to town and a visit to Liberty's, and soon the low, oak-beamed, lattice-windowed rooms began to be home. There was a jolly old-fashioned garden, with grass paths and no end of hollyhocks, and sunflowers, and big lilies, and roses with thousands of small sweet flowers. From the window you could see the marsh-pastures, and beyond them the blue, thin line of the sea. We were as happy as the summer was glorious, and settled down into work sooner than we ourselves expected. I was never tired of sketching the view and the wonderful cloud effects from the open lattice, and Laura would sit at the table and write verses about them, in which I mostly played the part of foreground.

We got a tall, old, peasant woman to do for us. Her face

and figure were good, though her cooking was of the homeliest; but she understood all about gardening, and told us all the old names of the coppices and cornfields, and the stories of the smugglers and the highwaymen, and, better still, of the 'things that walked,' and of the 'sights' which met one in lonely lanes of a starlight night. She was a great comfort to us, because Laura hated housekeeping as much as I loved folk-lore, and we soon came to leave all the domestic business to Mrs Dorman, and to use her legends in little magazine stories which brought in guineas.

We had three months of married happiness. We did not have a single quarrel. And then it happened. One October evening I had been down to smoke a pipe with the doctor – our only neighbour – a pleasant young Irishman. Laura had stayed at home to finish a comic sketch of a village episode for the *Monthly Marplot*. I left her laughing over her own jokes, and came in to see her a crumpled heap of pale muslin, weeping on the window seat.

'Good heavens, my darling, what's the matter?' I cried, taking her in my arms. She leaned her head against my shoulder, and went on crying. I had never seen her cry before – we had always been so happy, you see – and I felt sure some frightful misfortune had happened.

'What *is* the matter? Do speak!'

'It's Mrs Dorman,' she sobbed.

'What has she done?' I inquired, immensely relieved.

'She says she must go before the end of the month, and she says her niece is ill; she's gone down to see her now, but I don't believe that's the reason, because her niece is always ill. I believe someone has been setting her against us. Her manner was so queer –'

'Never mind, Pussy,' I said. 'Whatever you do, don't cry, or I shall have to cry, too, to keep you in countenance, and then you'll never respect your man again.'

She dried her eyes obediently on my handkerchief, and even smiled faintly.

'But, you see,' she went on, 'it is really serious, because

these village people are so sheepy; and if one won't do a thing, you may be sure none of the others will. And I shall have to cook the dinners and wash up all the hateful, greasy plates; and you'll have to carry cans of water about, and clean the boots and knives – and we shall never have any time for work, or earn any money or anything. We shall have to work all day, and only be able to rest when we are waiting for the kettle to boil!'

I represented to her that, even if we had to perform these duties, the day would still present some margin for other toils and recreations. But she refused to see the matter in any but the greyest light. She was very unreasonable, and I told her so, but in my heart ... well, who wants a woman to be reasonable?

'I'll speak to Mrs Dorman when she comes back, and see if I can't come to terms with her,' I said. 'Perhaps she wants a rise in her screw. It will be all right. Let's walk up to the church.'

The church was a large and lonely one, and we loved to go there, especially upon bright nights. The path skirted a wood, cut through it once, and ran along the crest of the hill through two meadows and round the churchyard wall, over which the old yews loomed in black masses of shadow. This path, which was partly paved, was called the 'bier-balk,' for it had long been the way by which the corpses had been carried to burial. The churchyard was richly treed, and was shaded by great elms, which stood just outside and stretched their kind arms out over the dead. A large, low porch let one into the building by a Norman doorway and a heavy oak door studded with iron. Inside, the arches rose into darkness, and between them shone the reticulated windows, which stood out white in the moonlight. In the chancel, the windows were of rich glass, which showed in faint light their noble colouring and made the black oak of the choir pews hardly more solid than the shadows. But on each side of the altar lay a grey marble figure of a knight in full armour, lying upon a low slab, with hands held up in everlasting prayer, and these figures, oddly enough, were always to be seen if there was any glimmer of light in the church. Their names were lost, but the peasants told of them that they had been fierce and wicked men, marauders by land and sea, who had been the scourge of their time, and had been guilty of deeds so foul that the house they had lived in – the big house, by the way, that had stood on the site of our cottage – had been stricken by lightning and the vengeance of Heaven. But for all that, the gold of their heirs had bought them a place in the church. Looking at the bad, hard faces reproduced in the marble, this story was easily believed.

The church looked at its best on that night, for the shadows of the yew trees fell through the windows upon the floor of the nave, and touched the pillars with tattered shadow. We sat down together without speaking, and watched the solemn beauty of the old church with some of that awe which inspired its early builders. We walked to the chancel and looked at the sleeping warriors. Then we rested on the stone seat in the porch, looking out over the stretch of quiet, moonlit meadows, feeling in every fibre of our being the peace of the night and of our happy love; and came away at last with a sense that even scrubbing and black-leading were, at their worst, but small troubles.

Mrs Dorman had come back from the village, and I at once invited her to a *tête-à-tête*.

'Now, Mrs Dorman,' I said, when I had got her into my painting-room, 'what's all this about your not staying with us?'

'I should be glad to get away, sir, before the end of the month,' she answered, with her usual placid dignity.

'Have you any fault to find, Mrs Dorman?'

'None at all, sir; you and your lady have always been most kind, I'm sure –'

'Well, what is it? Are your wages not high enough?'

'No, sir, I gets quite enough.'

'Then why not stay?'

'I'd rather not,' with some hesitation. 'My niece is ill.'

'But your niece has been ill ever since we came.'

No answer. There was a long and awkward silence. I broke it.

'Can't you stay for another month?' I asked.

'No, sir. I'm bound to go on Thursday.'

And this was Monday.

'Well, I must say, I think you might have let us know before. There's no time now to get anyone else, and your mistress is not fit to do heavy housework. Can't you stay till next week?'

'I might be able to come back next week.'

I was now convinced that all she wanted was a brief holiday, which we should have been willing enough to let her have, as soon as we could get a substitute.

'But why must you go this week?' I persisted. 'Come, out with it.'

Mrs Dorman drew the little shawl, which she always wore, tightly across her bosom, as though she were cold. Then she said, with a sort of effort:

'They say, sir, as this was a big house in Catholic times, and there was a many deeds done here.'

The nature of the 'deeds' might be vaguely inferred from the inflection of Mrs Dorman's voice, which was enough to make one's blood run cold. I was glad that Laura was not in the room. She was always nervous, as highly strung natures are, and I felt that these tales about our house, told by this old peasant woman with her impressive manner and contagious credulity, might have made our home less dear to my wife.

'Tell me all about it, Mrs Dorman,' I said. 'You needn't mind about telling me. I'm not like the young people, who make fun of such things.'

Which was partly true.

'Well, sir,' she sank her voice, 'you may have seen in the church, beside the altar, two shapes –'

'You mean the effigies of the knights in armour?' I said cheerfully.

'I mean them two bodies drawed out man-size in marble,' she returned; and I had to admit that her description was a thousand times more graphic than mine.

'They do say as on All Saints' Eve them two bodies sits up on their slabs and gets off of them, and then walks down the aisle *in their marble*' – (another good phrase, Mrs Dorman) – 'and as the church clock strikes eleven, they walks out of the church door, and over the graves, and along the bier-balk, and if it's a wet night there's the marks of their feet in the morning.'

'And where do they go?' I asked, rather fascinated.

'They comes back to their old home, sir, and if anyone meets them –'

'Well, what then?' I asked.

But no, not another word could I get from her, save that her niece was ill, and that she must go. After what I had heard I scorned to discuss the niece, and tried to get from Mrs Dorman more details of the legend. I could get nothing but warnings.

'Whatever you do, sir, lock the door early on All Saints' Eve, and make the blessed cross-sign over the doorstep and on the windows.'

'But has anyone ever seen these things?' I persisted.

'That's not for me to say. I know what I know.'

'Well, who was here last year?'

'No one, sir. The lady as owned the house only stayed here in the summer, and she always went to London a full month afore *the* night. And I'm sorry to inconvenience you and your lady, but my niece is ill, and I must go on Thursday.'

I could have shaken her for her reiteration of that obvious fiction.

She was determined to go, nor could our united entreaties move her in the least.

I did not tell Laura the legend of the shapes that 'walked

in their marble,' partly because a legend concerning our house might trouble my wife, and partly, I think, for some more occult reason. This was not quite the same to me as any other story, and I did not want to talk about it till the day was over. I had very soon almost ceased to think of the legend, however. I was painting a portrait of Laura, against the lattice window, and I could not think of much else. I had got a splendid background of yellow and grey sunset, and was working away with enthusiasm at her face. On Thursday Mrs Dorman went. She relented, at parting, so far as to say:

'Don't you put yourselves about too much, ma'am, and if there's any little thing I can do next week, I'm sure I shan't mind.'

From which I inferred that she wished to come back to us after Hallowe'en. Up to the last she adhered to the fiction of the niece.

Thursday passed off pretty well. Laura showed marked ability in the matter of steak and potatoes, and I confess that my knives, and the plates, which I insisted upon washing, were better done than I had dared to expect. It was all so good, so simple, so pleasant. As I write of it, I almost forget what came after. But now I must remember, and tell.

Friday came. It is about what happened on that Friday that this is written. I wonder if I should have believed it if anyone had told it to me. I will write the story of it as quickly and plainly as I can. Everything that happened on that day is burnt into my brain. I shall not forget anything, nor leave anything out.

I got up early, I remember, and lighted the kitchen fire, and had just achieved a smoky success, when my wife came running down, as sunny and sweet as the clear October morning itself. We prepared breakfast together, and found it very good fun. The housework was soon done, and when brushes and brooms and pails were quiet again, the house was still indeed. It is wonderful what a difference *one* makes in a house. We really missed Mrs Dorman, quite apart from considerations of pots and pans. We spent the day in dusting our books and putting them straight, and dined gaily on cold steak and coffee. Laura was, if possible, brighter and gayer and sweeter than usual, and I began to think that a little domestic toil was really good for her. We had never been so merry since we were married, and the walk we had that afternoon was, I think, the happiest time of all my life. When we had watched the deep scarlet clouds slowly pale into leaden grey against a pale-green sky, and saw the white mists curl up along the hedgerows in the distant marsh, we came back to the house, silently, hand in hand.

'You are sad, Pussy,' I said half-jestingly, as we sat down together in our little parlour. I expected a disclaimer, for my own silence had been the silence of complete happiness. To my surprise, she said:

'Yes, I think I am sad, or rather I am uneasy. I hope I am not going to be ill. I have shivered three or four times since we came in, and it's not really cold, is it?'

'No,' I said, and hoped it was not a chill caught from the treacherous marsh mists that roll up from the marshes in the dying light. No, she said, she did not think so. Then, after a silence, she spoke suddenly:

'Do you ever have presentiments of evil?'

'No,' I said, smiling; 'and I shouldn't believe in them if I had.'

'I do,' she went on; 'the night my father died I knew it, though he was right away in the north of Scotland.' I did not answer in words.

She sat looking at the fire in silence for some time, gently stroking my hand. At last she sprang up, came behind me, and drawing my head back, kissed me.

'There, it's over now,' she said. 'What a baby I am. Come, light the candles, and we'll have some of these new Rubinstein duets.'

And we spent a happy hour or two at the piano.

At about half-past ten, I began to fill the good-night pipe, but Laura looked so white that I felt that it would be brutal of me to fill our sitting-room with the fumes of strong cavendish.

'I'll take my pipe outside,' I said.

'Let me come too.'

'No, sweetheart, not tonight; you're much too tired. I shan't be long. Get to bed, or I shall have an invalid to nurse tomorrow, as well as the boots to clean.'

I kissed her and was turning to go, when she flung her arms round my neck and held me very closely. I stroked her hair.

'Come, Pussy, you're over-tired. The housework has been too much for you.'

She loosened her clasp a little and drew a deep breath.

'No. We've been very happy today, Jack, haven't we? Don't stay out too long.'

'I won't, Puss cat,' I said.

I strolled out of the front door, leaving it unlatched. What a night it was! The jagged masses of heavy, dark cloud were rolling at intervals from horizon to horizon, and thin, white wreaths covered the stars. Through all the rush of the cloud river, the moon swam, breasting the waves and disappearing again in the darkness. When, now and again, her light reached the woodlands, they seemed to be slowly and noiselessly waving in time to the clouds above them. There was a strange, grey light over all the earth; the fields had that shadowy bloom over them which only comes from the marriage of dew and moonshine, or frost and starlight.

I walked up and down, drinking in the beauty of the quiet earth and changing sky. The night was absolutely silent. Nothing seemed to be abroad. There was no scurrying of rabbits, or twitter of half-asleep birds. And though the clouds went sailing across the sky, the wind that drove them never came low enough to rustle the dead leaves in the woodland paths. Across the meadow, I could see the

church tower standing out black and grey against the sky.
I walked there, thinking over our three months of happiness, and of my wife – her dear eyes, her pretty ways. Oh,
my girl! my own little girl; what a vision came to me then
of a long, glad life for you and me together!

I heard a bell-beat from the church. Eleven already! I
turned to go in, but the night held me. I could not go back
into our little warm rooms yet. I would go right on up to
the church. I felt vaguely that it would be good to carry
my love and thankfulness to the sanctuary, whither so
many loads of sorrow and gladness had been borne by men
and women dead long since.

I looked in at the low window as I went by. Laura was
half lying on her chair in front of the fire. I could not see
her face, only her head showed dark against the pale blue
wall. She was quite still. Asleep, no doubt. My heart
reached out to her, as I went on. There must be a God, I
thought, and a God that was good. How otherwise could
anything so sweet and dear as she ever have been
imagined?

I walked slowly along the edge of the wood. A sound
broke the stillness of the night. I stopped and listened. The
sound stopped too. I went on, and now distinctly I heard
another step than mine answer mine like an echo. It was
a poacher or a wood-stealer, most likely, for these were not
unknown in our Arcadia. But, whoever it was, he was a
fool not to step more lightly. I turned into the wood, and
now the footstep seemed to come from the path I had just
left. It must be an echo, I thought. The wood lay lovely in
the moonlight. The large, dying ferns and the brushwood
showed where, through thinning foliage, the pale light
came down. The tree trunks stood up like Gothic columns
all around me. They reminded me of the church, and I
turned into the bier-balk and passed through the corpse-
gate between the graves to the low porch. I paused for a
moment on the stone seat where Laura and I had last
night watched the fading landscape. Then I noticed that

the door of the church was open, and I blamed myself for having left it unlatched the other night. We were the only people who ever cared to come to the church except on Sundays, and I was vexed to think that through our carelessness the damp autumn airs had had a chance of getting in and injuring the old fabric. I went in. It will seem strange perhaps that I should have gone half-way up the aisle before I remembered – with a sudden chill, followed by as sudden a rush of self-contempt – that this was the very day and hour when, according to tradition, the 'shapes drawed out man-size in marble,' began to walk.

Having thus remembered the legend, and remembered it with a shiver of which I was ashamed, I could not do otherwise than walk up towards the altar, just to look at the figures – as I said to myself; really what I wanted was to assure myself, first, that I did not believe the legend, and, secondly, that it was not true. I was rather glad that I had come. I thought that now I could tell Mrs Dorman how vain her fancies were, and how peacefully the marble figures slept on through the ghostly hour. With my hands in my pockets, I passed up the aisle. In the grey, dim light, the eastern end of the church looked larger than usual, and the arches above the tombs looked larger too. The moon came out and showed me the reason. I stopped short, my heart gave a great leap that nearly choked me, and then sank sickeningly.

The 'bodies drawed out man-size' *were gone*, and their marble slabs lay wide and bare in the vague moonlight that slanted through the west window.

Were they really gone? or was I mad? Clenching my nerves, I stooped and passed my hand over the smooth slabs and felt their flat unbroken surface. Had someone taken the things away? Was is some vile practical joke? I would make sure, anyway. In an instant I had made a torch of a newspaper which happened to be in my pocket, and lighting it held it high above my head. Its yellow glare illumined the dark arches and those slabs.

The figures *were* gone. And I was alone in the church; or was I alone?

And then a horror seized me, a horror indefinable and indescribable – an overwhelming certainty of supreme and accomplished calamity. I flung down the torch and tore along the aisle and out through the door, biting my lips as I ran to keep myself from shrieking aloud. Was I mad – or what was this that possessed me? I leaped the churchyard wall and took the straight cut across the fields, led by the light from our windows. Just as I got over the first stile, a dark figure seemed to spring out of the ground. Mad still with the certainty of misfortune, I made for the thing that stood in my path, shouting 'Get out of the way, can't you?'

But my push met with a very vigorous resistance. My arms were caught just above the elbow and held as in a vice, and the raw-boned Irish doctor actually shook me.

'Would ye?' he cried in his own unmistakable accents – 'would ye, then?'

'Let me go, you fool,' I gasped. 'The marble figures have gone from the church; I tell you they've gone.'

He broke into a ringing laugh. 'I'll have to give ye a draught tomorrow, I see. Ye've been smoking too much and listening to old wives' tales.'

'I tell you I've seen the bare slabs.'

'Well, come back with me. I'm going up to old Palmer's – his daughter's ill – it's only hysteria, but it's as bad as it can be; we'll look in at the church and let *me* see the bare slabs.'

'You go if you like,' I said, a little less frantic for his laughter, 'I'm going home to my wife.'

'Rubbish, man,' said he; 'd'ye think I'll permit of that? Are ye to go saying all yer life that ye've seen solid marble endowed with vitality, and me to go all my life saying ye were a coward? No, sir – ye shan't do ut!'

The quiet night – a human voice – and I think also the physical contact with this six feet of solid common sense, brought me back a little to my ordinary self, and the word 'coward' was a shower-bath.

'Come on, then,' I said sullenly, 'perhaps you're right.'

He still held my arm tightly. We got over the stile and back to the church. All was still as death. The place smelt very damp and earthy. We walked up the aisle. I am not ashamed to confess I shut my eyes; I knew the figures would not be there, I heard Kelly strike a match.

'Here they are, ye see, right enough; ye've been dreaming or drinking, asking yer pardon for the imputation.'

I opened my eyes. By Kelly's expiring vesta I saw two shapes lying 'in their marble' on their slabs. I drew a deep breath and caught his hand.

'I'm awfully indebted to you,' I said. 'It must have been some trick of light, or I have been working rather hard, perhaps that's it. Do you know, I was quite convinced they were gone.'

'I'm aware of that,' he answered rather grimly; 'ye'll have to be careful of that brain of yours, my friend, I assure you.'

He was leaning over and looking at the right-hand figure, whose stony face was the most villainous and deadly in expression. He struck another match.

'By Jove!' he said, 'something has been going on here – this hand is broken.'

And so it was. I was certain that it had been perfect the last time Laura and I had been there.

'Perhaps someone had *tried* to remove them,' said the young doctor.

'That won't account for my impression,' I objected.

'Too much painting and tobacco will account for what you call your impression,' he said.

'Come along,' I said, 'or my wife will be getting anxious. You'll come in and have a drop of whisky, and drink confusion to ghosts and better sense to me.'

'I ought to go up to Palmer's, but it's so late now, I'd best leave it till the morning,' he replied. 'I was kept late at the Union, and I've had to see a lot of people since. All right, I'll come back with ye.'

I think he fancied I needed him more than did Palmer's girl, so, discussing how such an illusion could have been possible, and deducing from this experience large generalities concerning ghostly apparitions, we saw, as we walked up the garden path, that bright light streamed out of the front door, and presently saw that the parlour door was open too. Had she gone out?

' 'Come in,' I said, and Dr Kelly followed me into the parlour. It was all ablaze with candles, not only the wax ones, but at least a dozen guttering, glaring, tallow dips, stuck in vases and ornaments in unlikely places. Light, I knew, was Laura's remedy for nervousness. Poor child! Why had I left her? Brute that I was.

We glanced round the room, and at first we did not see her. The window was open and the draught set all the candles flaring one way. Her chair was empty, and her handkerchief and book lay on the floor. I turned to the window. There, in the recess of the window, I saw her. Oh, my child, my love, had she gone to that window to watch for me? And what had come into the room behind her? To what had she turned with that look of frantic fear and horror? Had she thought that it was my step she heard and turned to meet – what?

She had fallen back against a table in the window, and her body lay half on it and half on the window-seat, and her head hung down over the table, the brown hair loosened and fallen to the carpet. Her lips were drawn back and her eyes wide, wide open. They saw nothing now. What had they last seen?

The doctor moved towards her. But I pushed him aside and sprang to her; caught her in my arms, and cried –

'It's all right, Laura! I've got you safe, dear!'

She fell into my arms in a heap. I clasped her and kissed her, and called her by all her pet names, but I think I knew all the time that she was dead. Her hands were tightly clenched. In one of them she held something fast. When I was quite sure that she was dead, and that nothing mattered at all any more, I let him open her hand to see what she held.

It was a grey marble finger.

THE VIOLET CAR

Do you know the downs – the wide windy spaces, the rounded shoulders of the hills leaned against the sky, the hollows where farms and homesteads nestle sheltered, with trees round them pressed close and tight as a carnation in a button-hole? On long summer days it is good to lie on the downs, between short turf and pale, clear sky, to smell the wild thyme, and hear the tiny tinkle of the sheep-bells and the song of the skylark. But on winter evenings when the wind is waking up to its work, spitting rain in your eyes, beating the poor, naked trees and shaking the dusk across the hills like a gray pall, then it is better to be by a warm fireside, in one of the farms that lie lonely where shelter is, and oppose their windows glowing with candle light and firelight to the deepening darkness, as faith holds up its love-lamp in the night of sin and sorrow that is life.

I am unaccustomed to literary effort, and I feel that I shall not say what I have to say, or that it will convince you, unless I say it very plainly. I thought I could adorn my story with pleasant words, prettily arranged. But as I pause to think of what really happened, I see that the plainest words will be the best. I do not know how to weave a plot, nor how to embroider it. It is best not to try. These things happened. I have no skill to add to what happened; nor is any adding of mine needed.

I am a nurse – and I was sent for to go to Charlestown – a mental case. It was November and the fog was thick in London, so that my cab went at a foot's pace, so I missed the train by which I should have gone. I sent a telegram to Charlestown, and waited in the dismal waiting room at London Bridge. The time was passed for me by a little child. Its mother, a widow, seemed too crushed to be able to respond to its quick questionings. She answered briefly, and not, as it seemed, to the child's satisfaction. The child itself presently seemed to perceive that its mother was not, so to speak, available. It leaned back on the wide, dusty seat and yawned. I caught its eye, and smiled. It would not smile, but it looked. I took out of my bag a silk purse, bright with beads and steel tassels, and turned it over and over. Presently, the child slid along the seat and said, 'Let me.' After that all was easy. The mother sat with eyes closed. When I rose to go, she opened them and thanked me. The child, clinging, kissed me. Later, I saw them get into a first class carriage in my train. My ticket was a third class one.

I expected, of course, that there would be a conveyance of some sort to meet me at the station, but there was nothing. Nor was there a cab or a fly to be seen. It was by this time nearly dark, and the wind was driving the rain almost horizontally along the unfrequented road that lay beyond the door of the station. I looked out, forlorn and perplexed.

'Haven't you engaged a carriage?' It was the widow lady who spoke.

I explained.

'My motor will be here directly,' she said, 'you'll let me drive you? Where is it you are going?'

'Charlestown,' I said, and as I said it, I was aware of a very odd change in her face. A faint change, but quite unmistakable.

'Why do you look like that?' I asked her bluntly. And, of course, she said, 'Like what?'

'There's nothing wrong with the house?' I said, for that, I found, was what I had taken that faint change to signify; and I was very young, and one has heard tales. 'No reason why I shouldn't go there, I mean?'

'No – oh no –' she glanced out through the rain, and I knew as well as though she had told me that there was a reason why *she* should not wish to go there.

'Don't trouble,' I said, 'it's very kind of you but it's probably out of your way and . . .'

'Oh, but I'll take you – of *course* I'll take you,' she said, and the child said, 'Mother, here comes the car.'

And come it did, though neither of us heard it till the child had spoken. I know nothing of motor cars, and I don't know the names of any of the parts of them. This was like a brougham – only you got in at the back, as you do in a waggonette; the seats were in the corners, and when the door was shut there was a little seat that pulled up, and the child sat on it between us. And it moved like magic, or like a dream of a train.

We drove quickly through the dark. I could hear the wind screaming, and the wild dashing of the rain against the windows, even through the whirring of the machinery. One could see nothing of the country, only the black night, and the shafts of light from the lamps in front.

After, as it seemed, a very long time, the chauffeur got down and opened a gate. We went through it, and after that the road was very much rougher. We were quite silent in the car, and the child had fallen asleep.

We stopped, and the car stood pulsating, as though it were out of breath, while the chauffeur hauled down my box. It was so dark that I could not see the shape of the house, only the lights in the downstairs windows, and the low-walled front garden faintly revealed by their light and the light of the motor lamps. Yet I felt that it was a fair-sized house, that it was surrounded by big trees, and that there was a pond or river close by. In daylight next day I found that all this was so. I have never been able to tell how I knew it that first night, in the dark, but I did know it. Perhaps there was something in the way the rain fell on the trees and on the water. I don't know.

The chauffeur took my box up a stone path, whereon I got out, and said my goodbyes and thanks.

'Don't wait, please, don't,' I said. 'I'm all right now. Thank you a thousand times!'

The car, however, stood pulsating till I had reached the doorstep, then it caught its breath, as it were, throbbed more loudly, turned, and went.

And still the door had not opened. I felt for the knocker, and rapped smartly. Inside the door I was sure I heard whispering. The car light was fast diminishing to a little distant star, and its panting sounded now hardly at all. When it ceased to sound at all, the place was quiet as death. The lights glowed redly from curtained windows, but there was no other sign of life. I wished I had not been in such a hurry to part from my escort, from human companionship, and from the great, solid, competent presence of the motor car.

I knocked again, and this time I followed the knock by a shout.

'Hullo!' I cried. 'Let me in. I'm the nurse!'

There was a pause, such a pause as would allow time for whisperers to exchange glances on the other side of a door.

Then a bolt ground back, a key turned, and the doorway framed no longer cold, wet wood, but light and a welcoming warmth – and faces.

'Come in, oh, come in,' said a voice, a woman's voice, and the voice of a man said: 'We didn't know there was anyone there.'

And I had shaken the very door with my knockings!

I went in, blinking at the light, and the man called a servant, and between them they carried my box upstairs.

The woman took my arm and led me into a low, square room, pleasant, homely, and comfortable, with solid mid-Victorian comfort – the kind that expressed itself in rep and mahogany. In the lamplight I turned to look at her. She was small and thin, her hair, her face, and her hands were of the same tint of greyish yellow.

'Mrs Eldridge?' I asked.

'Yes,' said she, very softly. 'Oh! I am so glad you've come. I hope you won't be dull here. I hope you'll stay. I hope I shall be able to make you comfortable.'

She had a gentle, urgent way of speaking that was very winning.

'I'm sure I shall be very comfortable,' I said; 'but it's I that am to take care of you. Have you been ill long?'

'It's not me that's ill, really,' she said, 'it's him –'

Now, it was Mr Robert Eldridge who had written to engage me to attend on his wife, who was, he said, slightly deranged.

'I see.' said I. One must never contradict them; it only aggravates their disorder.

'The reason ...' she was beginning, when his foot sounded on the stairs, and she fluttered off to get candles and hot water.

He came in and shut the door – A fair bearded, elderly man, quite ordinary.

'You'll take care of her,' he said. 'I don't want her to get talking to people. She fancies things.'

'What form do the illusions take?' I asked, prosaically.

'She thinks I'm mad,' he said, with a short laugh.

'It's a very usual form. Is that all?'

'It's about enough. And she can't hear things that I can hear, see things that I can see, and she can't smell things. By the way, you didn't see or hear anything of a motor as you came up, did you?'

'I came up *in* a motor car,' I said shortly. 'You never sent to meet me, and a lady gave me a lift.' I was going to explain about my missing the earlier train, when I found that he was not listening to me. He was watching the door. When his wife came in, with a steaming jug in one hand and a flat candlestick in the other, he went towards her, and whispered eagerly. The only words I caught were: 'She came in a real motor.'

Apparently, to these simple people a motor was as great a novelty as to me. My telegram, by the way, was delivered next morning.

They were very kind to me; they treated me as an honoured guest. When the rain stopped, as it did late the next day, and I was able to go out, I found that Charlestown was a farm, a large farm, but even to my inexperienced eyes it seemed neglected and unprosperous. There was absolutely nothing for me to do but to follow Mrs Eldridge, helping her where I could in her household duties, and to sit with her while she sewed in the homely parlour. When I had been in the house a few days, I began to put together the little things that I had noticed singly, and the life at the farm seemed suddenly to come into focus, as strange surroundings do after a while.

I found that I had noticed that Mr and Mrs Eldridge were very fond of each other, and that it was a fondness, and their way of showing it was a way that told that they had known sorrow, and had borne it together. That she showed no sign of mental derangement, save in the persistent belief of hers that *he* was deranged. That the morning found them fairly cheerful; that after the early dinner they seemed to grow more and more depressed; that after the 'early cup of tea' – that is just as dusk was falling – they always went for a walk together. That they never asked me to join them in this walk, and that it always took the same direction – across the downs towards the sea. That they always returned from this walk pale and dejected; that she sometimes cried afterwards alone in their bedroom, while he was shut up in the little room they called the office, where he did his accounts, and paid his men's wages, and where his hunting-crops and guns were kept. After supper, which was early, they always made an effort to be cheerful. I knew that this effort was for my sake, and I knew that each of them thought it was good for the other to make it.

Just as I had known before they showed it to me that Charlestown was surrounded by big trees and had a great pond beside it, so I knew, and in as inexplicable a way, that with these two fear lived. It looked at me out of their eyes. And I knew, too, that this fear was not her fear. I had not been two days in the place before I found that I was beginning to be fond of them both. They were so kind, so gentle, so ordinary, so homely – the kind of people who ought not to have known the name of fear – the kind of people to whom all honest, simple joys should have come by right, and no sorrows but such as come to us all, the death of old friends, and the slow changes of advancing years.

They seemed to belong to the land – to the downs, and the copses, and the old pastures, and the lessening corn-fields. I found myself wishing that I, too, belonged to these, that I had been born a farmer's daughter. All the stress and struggle of cram and exam, of school, and college, and hospital, seemed so loud and futile, compared with these open secrets of the down life. And I felt this the more, as more and more I felt that I must leave it all – that there was, honestly, no work for me here such as for good or ill I had been trained to do.

'I ought not to stay,' I said to her one afternoon, as we stood at the open door. It was February now, and the snowdrops were thick in tufts beside the flagged path. 'You are quite well.'

'*I* am,' she said.

'You are quite well, both of you,' I said. 'I oughtn't to be taking your money and doing nothing for it.'

'You're doing everything,' she said; 'you don't know how much you're doing.'

'We had a daughter of our own once,' she added vaguely, and then, after a very long pause, she said very quietly and distinctly:

'He has never been the same since.'

'How not the same?' I asked, turning my face up to the thin February sunshine.

She tapped her wrinkled, yellow-grey forehead, as country people do.

'Not right here,' she said.

'How?' I asked. 'Dear Mrs Eldridge, tell me; perhaps I could help somehow.'

Her voice was so sane, so sweet. It had come to this with me, that I did not know which of those two was the one who needed my help.

'He sees things that no one else sees, and hears things no one else hears, and smells things that you can't smell if you're standing there beside him.'

I remembered with a sudden smile his words to me on the evening of my arrival:

'She can't see, or hear, or smell.'

And once more I wondered to which of the two I owed my service.

'Have you any idea why?' I asked. She caught at my arm.

'It was after our Bessie died,' she said—'the very day she was buried. The motor that killed her—they said it was an accident—it was on the Brighton Road. It was a violet colour. They go into mourning for queens with violet, don't they?' she added; 'and my Bessie, she was a queen. So the motor was violet. That was all right, wasn't it?'

I told myself now that I saw that the woman was not normal, and I saw why. It was grief that had turned her brain. There must have been some change in my look, though I ought to have known better, for she said suddenly, 'No I'll not tell you any more.'

And then he came out. He never left me alone with her for very long. Nor did she ever leave him for very long alone with me.

I did not intend to spy upon them, though I am not sure that my position as nurse to one mentally afflicted would not have justified such spying. But I did not spy. It was chance. I had been to the village to get some blue sewing silk for a blouse I was making, and there was a royal sunset which tempted me to prolong my walk. That was how I found myself on the high downs where they slope to the broken edge of England—the sheer, white cliffs against which the English Channel beats for ever. The furze was in flower, and the skylarks were singing, and my thoughts

were with my own life, my own hopes and dreams. So I
found that I had struck a road, without knowing when I
had struck it. I followed it towards the sea, and quite soon
it ceased to be a road, and merged in the pathless turf as a
stream sometimes disappears in sand. There was nothing
but turf and furze bushes, the song of the skylarks, and
beyond the slope that ended at the cliff's edge, the booming
of the sea. I turned back, following the road, which defined
itself again a few yards back, and presently sank to a lane,
deep-banked and bordered with brown hedge stuff. It was
there that I came upon them in the dusk. And I heard
their voices before I saw them, and before it was possible
for them to see me. It was her voice that I heard first.

'No, no, no, no, no,' it said.

'I tell you yes,' that was his voice; 'there – can't you hear
it, that panting sound – right away – away? It must be at
the very edge of the cliff.'

'There's nothing, dearie,' she said, 'indeed there's nothing.'

'You're deaf – and blind – stand back I tell you, it's
close upon us.'

I came round the corner of the lane then, and as I came,
I saw him catch her arm and throw her against the hedge
– violently, as though the danger he feared were indeed
close upon them. I stopped behind the turn of the hedge
and stepped back. They had not seen me. Her eyes were
on his face, and they held a world of pity, love, agony – his
face was set in a mask of terror, and his eyes moved quickly
as though they followed down the lane the swift passage of
something – something that neither she nor I could see.
Next moment he was cowering, pressing his body into the
hedge – his face hidden in his hands, and his whole body
trembling so that I could see it, even from where I was a
dozen yards away, through the light screen of the over-
grown hedge.

'And the smell of it!' he said, 'do you mean to tell me
you can't smell it?'

She had her arms round him.

'Come home, dearie,' she said. 'Come home! It's all your fancy – come home with your old wife that loves you.'

They went home.

Next day I asked her to come to my room to look at the new blue blouse. When I had shown it to her I told her, what I had seen and heard yesterday in the lane.

'And now I know,' I said, 'which of you it is that wants care.'

To my amazement she said very eagerly, 'Which?'

'Why, he – of course' I told her, 'there was nothing there.'

She sat down in the chintz-covered armchair by the window, and broke into wild weeping. I stood by her and soothed her as well as I could.

'It's a comfort to know,' she said at last, 'I haven't known what to believe. Many a time, lately, I've wondered whether after all it could be me that was mad, like he said. And there was nothing there? There always *was* nothing there – and it's on him the judgment, not on me. On him. Well, that's something to be thankful for.'

So her tears, I told myself, had been more of relief at her own escape. I looked at her with distaste, and forgot that I had been fond of her. So that her next words cut me like little knives.

'It's bad enough for him as it is,' she said – 'but it's nothing to what it would be for him, if I was really to go off my head and him left to think he'd brought it on me. You see, now I can look after him the same as I've always done. It's only once in the day it comes over him. He couldn't bear it, if it was all the time – like it'll be for me now. It's much better it should be him – I'm better able to bear it than he is.'

I kissed her then and put my arms round her, and said, 'Tell me what it is that frightens him so – and it's every day, you say?'

'Yes – ever since. I'll tell you. It's a sort of comfort to

speak out. It was a violet-coloured car that killed our Bessie. You know our girl that I've told you about. And it's a violet coloured car that he thinks he sees – every day up there in the lane. And he says he hears it, and that he smells the smell of the machinery – the stuff they put in it – you know.'

'Petrol?'

'Yes, and you can *see* he hears it, and you can *see* he sees it. It haunts him, as if it was a ghost. You see, it was he that picked her up after the violet car went over her. It was that that turned him. I only saw her as he carried her in, in his arms – and then he'd covered her face. But he saw her just as they'd left her, lying in the dust ... you could see the place on the road where it happened for days and days.'

'Didn't they come back?'

'Oh yes ... they came back. But Bessie didn't come back. But there was a judgment on them. The very night of the funeral, that violet car went over the cliff – dashed to pieces – every soul in it. That was the man's widow that drove you home the first night.'

'I wonder she uses a car after that,' I said. I wanted something commonplace to say.

'Oh,' said Mrs Eldridge, 'it's all what you're used to. We don't stop walking because our girl was killed on the road. Motoring comes as natural to them as walking to us. There's my old man calling – poor old dear. He wants me to go out with him.'

She went, all in a hurry, and in her hurry slipped on the stairs and twisted her ankle. It all happened in a minute and it was a bad sprain.

When I had bound it up, and she was on the sofa, she looked at him, standing as if he were undecided, staring out of the window with his cap in his hand. And she looked at me.

'Mr Eldridge mustn't miss his walk,' she said. 'You go with him, my dear. A breath of air will do you good.'

So I went, understanding as well as though he had told me, that he did not want me with him, and that he was afraid to go alone, and that he yet had to go.

We went up the lane in silence. At that corner he stopped suddenly, caught my arm, and dragged me back. His eyes followed something that I could not see. Then he exhaled a held breath, and said, 'I thought I heard a motor coming.' He had found it hard to control his terror, and I saw beads of sweat on his forehead and temples. Then we went back to the house.

The sprain was a bad one. Mrs Eldridge had to rest, and again next day it was I who went with him to the corner of the lane.

This time he could not, or did not try to, conceal what he felt. 'There – listen!' he said. 'Surely you can hear it?'

I heard nothing.

'Stand back,' he cried shrilly, suddenly, and we stood back close against the hedge.

Again the eyes followed something invisible to me, and again the held breath exhaled.

'It will kill me one of these days,' he said, 'and I don't know that I care how soon – if it wasn't for her.'

'Tell me,' I said, full of that importance, that conscious competence, that one feels in the presence of other people's troubles. He looked at me.

'I will tell you, by God,' he said. 'I couldn't tell *her*. Young lady, I've gone so far as wishing myself a Roman, for the sake of a priest to tell it to. But I can tell *you*, without losing my soul more than it's lost already. Did you ever hear tell of a violet car that got smashed up – went over the cliff?'

'Yes', I said. 'Yes.'

'The man that killed my girl was new to the place. And he hadn't any eyes – or ears – or he'd have known me, seeing we'd been face to face at the inquest. And you'd have thought he'd have stayed at home that one day, with the blinds drawn down. But not he. He was swirling and swivelling all about the country in his cursed violet car, the very time we were burying her. And at dusk – there was a mist coming up – he comes up behind me in this very lane; and I stood back, and he pulls up, and he calls out, with his damned lights full in my face:

' "Can you tell me the way to Hexham, my man?" says he.

'I'd have liked to show him the way to hell. And that was the way for me, not him. I don't know how I came to do it. I didn't mean to do it. I didn't think I was going to – and before I knew anything, I'd said it. "Straight ahead," I said; "keep straight ahead." Then the motor-thing panted, chuckled, and he was off. I ran after him to try to stop him – but what's the use of running after these motor-devils? And he kept straight on. And every day since then, every dear day, the car comes by, the violet car that nobody can see but me – and it keeps straight on.'

'You ought to go away,' I said, speaking as I had been trained to speak. 'You fancy these things. You probably fancied the whole thing. I don't suppose you ever *did* tell the violet car to go straight ahead. I expect it was all imagination, and the shock of your poor daughter's death. You ought to go right away.'

'I can't,' he said earnestly. 'If I did, someone else would see the car. You see, somebody *has* to see it every day as long as I live. If it wasn't me, it would be someone else. And I'm the only person who *deserves* to see it. I wouldn't like any one else to see it – it's too horrible. *It's* much more horrible than you think,' he added slowly.

I asked him, walking beside him down the quiet lane, what it was that was so horrible about the violet car. I think I quite expected him to say that it was splashed with his daughter's blood ... What he did say was, 'It's too horrible to tell you,' and he shuddered.

I was young then, and youth always thinks it can move mountains. I persuaded myself that I could cure him of his delusion by attacking – not the main fort – that is always,

to begin with, impregnable, but one, so to speak, of the outworks. I set myself to persuade him not to go to that corner in the lane, at that hour in the afternoon.

'But if I don't, someone else will see it.'

'There'll be nobody there *to* see it,' I said briskly.

'Someone will be there. Mark my words, someone will be there - and then they'll know.'

'Then I'll be the someone,' I said. 'Come - you stay at home with your wife, and *I'll* go - and if I see it I'll promise to tell you, and if I don't - well, then I will be able to go away with a clear conscience.'

'A clear conscience,' he repeated.

I argued with him in every moment when it was possible to catch him alone. I put all my will and all my energy into my persuasions. Suddenly, like a door that you've been trying to open, and that has resisted every key till the last one, he gave way. Yes - I should go to the lane. And he would not go.

I went.

Being, as I said before, a novice in the writing of stories, I perhaps haven't made you understand that it was quite hard for me to go - that I felt myself at once a coward and a heroine. This business of an imaginary motor that only one poor old farmer could see, probably appears to you quite commonplace and ordinary. It was not so with me. You see, the idea of this thing had dominated my life for weeks and months, had dominated it even before I knew the nature of the domination. It was this that was the fear that I had known to walk with these two people, the fear that shared their bed and board, that lay down and rose up with them. The old man's fear of this and his fear of his fear. And the old man was terribly convincing. When one talked with him, it was quite difficult to believe that he was mad, and that there wasn't, and couldn't be, a mysteriously horrible motor that was visible to him, and invisible to other people. And when he said that, if he were not in the lane, someone else would see it - it was easy to say 'Nonsense,' but to think 'Nonsense' was not so easy, and to *feel* 'Nonsense' quite oddly difficult.

I walked up and down the lane in the dusk, wishing not to wonder what might be the hidden horror in the violet car. I would not let blood into my thoughts. I was not going to be fooled by thought transference, or any of those transcendental follies. I was not going to be hypnotised into seeing things.

I walked up the lane - I had promised him to stand near that corner for five minutes, and I stood there in the deepening dusk, looking up towards the downs and the sea. There were pale stars. Everything was very still. Five minutes is a long time. I held my watch in my hand. Four - four and a half - four and three-quarters. Five. I turned instantly. And then I saw that *he* had followed me   he was standing a dozen yards away - and his face was turned from me. It was turned towards a motor car that shot up the lane - It came very swiftly, and before it came to where he was, I knew that it was very horrible. I crushed myself back into the crackling bare hedge, as I should have done to leave room for the passage of a real car - though I knew that this one was not real. It looked real - but I knew it was not.

As it neared him, he started back, then suddenly he cried out. I heard him. 'No, no, no, no - no more, no more,' was what he cried, with that he flung himself down on the road in front of the car, and its great tyres passed over him. Then the car shot past me and I saw what the full horror of it was. There was no blood - that was not the horror. The colour of it was, as she had said, violet.

I got to him and got his head up. He was dead. I was quite calm and collected now, and felt that to be so was extremely creditable to me. I went to a cottage where a labourer was having tea - he got some men and a hurdle.

When I had told his wife, the first intelligible thing she said was: 'It's better for him. Whatever he did he's paid for now - ' So it looks as though she had known - or guessed – more than he thought.

I stayed with her till her death. She did not live long.

You think perhaps that the old man was knocked down and killed by a real motor, which happened to come that way of all ways, at that hour of all hours, and happened to be, of all colours, violet. Well, a real motor leaves its mark on you where it kills you, doesn't it? But when I lifted up that old man's head from the road, there was no mark on him, no blood – no broken bones – his hair was not disordered, nor his dress. I tell you there was not even a speck of mud on him, except where he had touched the road in falling. There were no tyre-marks in the mud.

The motor car that killed him came and went like a shadow. As he threw himself down, it swerved a little so that both its wheels should go over him.

He died, the doctor said, of heart-failure. I am the only person to know that he was killed by a violet car, which, having killed him, went noiselessly away towards the sea. And that car was empty – there was no one in it. It was just a violet car that moved along the lanes swiftly and silently, and was empty.

JOHN CHARRINGTON'S WEDDING

No one ever thought that May Foster would marry John Charrington; but he thought differently, and things which John Charrington intended should happen had a way of happening. He asked her to marry him before he went up to Oxford. She laughed and refused him. He asked her again next time he came home. Again she laughed, tossed her blonde head, and again refused. A third time he asked her; she said it was becoming a confirmed habit, and laughed at him more than ever.

John was not the only man who wanted to marry her; she was the belle of our village, and we were all in love with her more or less; it was a sort of fashion, like heliotrope ties or Inverness capes. Therefore we were as much annoyed as surprised when John Charrington walked into our little local club – we held it in a loft over the saddler's, I remember – and invited us all to his wedding.

'Your wedding?'

'You don't mean it?'

'Who's the happy pair? When's it to be?'

John Charrington filled his pipe and lighted it before he replied. Then he said:

'I'm sorry to deprive you fellows of your only joke, but Miss Foster and I are to be married in September.'

'You don't mean it?'

'He's got the mitten again, and it's turned his head.'

'No,' I said, rising, 'I see it's true. Lend me a pistol someone, or a first-class fare to the other end of Nowhere. Charrington has bewitched the only pretty girl in our twenty-mile radius. Was it mesmerism, or a love-potion, Jack?'

'Neither, sir, but a gift you'll never have   perseverance and the best luck a man ever had in this world.'

There was something in his voice that silenced me, and all chaff of the other fellows failed to draw him further.

The queer thing about it was that, when we congratulated Miss Foster, she blushed, and smiled, and dimpled, for all the world as though she were in love with him and had been in love with him all the time. Upon my word, I think she had. Women are strange creatures.

We were all asked to the wedding. In Brixham, everyone who was anybody knew everybody else who was anyone. My sisters were, I truly believe, more interested in the *trousseau* than the bride herself, and I was to be best man. The coming marriage was much canvassed at afternoon tea-tables, and at our little club over the saddler's; and the question was always asked: 'Does she care for him?'

I used to ask that question myself in the early days of their engagement, but after a certain evening in August I never asked it again. I was coming home from the club through the churchyard. Our church is on a thyme-grown hill, and the turf about it is so thick and soft that one's footsteps are noiseless.

I made no sound as I vaulted the low wall and threaded my way between the tombstones. It was at the same instant that I heard John Charrington's voice and saw her. May was sitting on a low, flat gravestone, her face turned towards the full splendour of the setting sun. Its expression ended, at once and for ever, any question of love for him; it was transfigured to a beauty I should not have believed possible, even to that beautiful little face.

John lay at her feet, and it was his voice that broke the stillness of the golden August evening.

'My dear, I believe I should come back to you from the dead, if you wanted me!'

I coughed at once to indicate my presence, and passed on into the shadow fully enlightened.

The wedding was to be early in September. Two days

before, I had to run up to town on business. The train was late, of course, for we were on the South-Eastern, and as I stood grumbling with my watch in my hand, whom should I see but John Charrington and May Foster. They were walking up and down the unfrequented end of the platform, arm-in-arm, looking into each other's eyes, careless of the sympathetic interest of the porters.

Of course I knew better than to hesitate a moment before burying myself in the booking-office, and it was not till the train drew up at the platform that I obtrusively passed the pair with my Gladstone, and took the corner in a first-class smoking-carriage. I did this with as good an air of not seeing them as I could assume. I pride myself on my discretion, but if John were travelling alone, I wanted his company. I had it.

'Hullo, old man,' came his cheery voice, as he swung his bag into my carriage, 'here's luck. I was expecting a dull journey.'

'Where are you off to?' I asked, discretion still bidding me turn my eyes away, though I saw, without looking, that hers were red-rimmed.

'To old Branbridge's,' he answered, shutting the door, and leaning out for a last word with his sweetheart.

'Oh, I wish you wouldn't go, John,' she was saying in a low, earnest voice. 'I feel certain something will happen.'

'Do you think I should let anything happen to keep me, and the day after tomorrow our wedding-day?'

'Don't go,' she answered, with a pleading intensity that would have sent my Gladstone on to the platform, and me after it. But she wasn't speaking to me. John Charrington was made differently – he rarely changed his opinions, never his resolutions.

He just touched the ungloved hands that lay on the carriage door.

'I must, May. The old boy has been awfully good to me, and now he's dying I must go and see him, but I shall come home in time – ' The rest of the parting was lost in a whisper and the rattling lurch of the starting train.

'You're sure to come?' she spoke, as the train moved.

'Nothing shall keep me,' he answered, and we steamed out. After he had seen the last of the little figure on the platform, he leaned back in his corner and kept silence for a minute.

When he spoke it was to explain to me that his god-father, whose heir he was, lay dying at Peasemarsh Place, some fifty miles away, and he had sent for John, and John had felt bound to go.

'I shall be surely back tomorrow,' he said, 'or, if not, the day after, in heaps of time. Thank Heaven, one hasn't to get up in the middle of the night to get married nowadays.'

'And suppose Mr Branbridge dies?'

'Alive or dead, I mean to be married on Thursday!' John answered, lighting a cigar and unfolding *The Times*.

At Peasemarsh station we said 'good-bye,' and he got out, and I saw him ride off. I went on to London, where I stayed the night.

When I got home the next afternoon, a very wet one, by the way, my sister greeted me with:

'Where's Mr Charrington?'

'Goodness knows,' I answered testily. Every man since Cain has resented that kind of question.

'I thought you might have heard from him,' she went on, 'as you're to give him away tomorrow.'

'Isn't he back?' I asked, for I had confidently expected to find him at home.

'No, Geoffrey' – my sister always had a way of jumping to conclusions, especially such conclusions as were least favourable to her fellow creatures – 'he has not returned, and, what is more, you may depend upon it, he won't. You mark my words, there'll be no wedding tomorrow.'

My sister Fanny has a power of annoying me which no other human being possesses.

'You mark my words,' I retorted with asperity, 'you had better give up making such a thundering idiot of yourself.

There'll be more wedding tomorrow than ever you'll take first part in.'

But though I could snarl confidently to my sister, I did not feel so comfortable when, late that night, standing on the doorstep of John's house, I heard that he had not returned. I went home gloomily through the rain. Next morning brought a brilliant blue sky, gold sun, and all such softness of air and beauty of cloud as go to make a perfect day. I woke with a vague feeling of having gone to bed anxious, and of being rather averse from facing that anxiety in the light of full wakefulness.

With my shaving-water came a letter from John which relieved my mind, and sent me up to the Fosters with a light heart.

May was in the garden. I saw her blue gown among the hollyhocks as the lodge gates swung to behind me. So I did not go up to the house, but turned aside down the turfed path.

'He's written to you too,' she said, without preliminary greeting, when I reached her side.

'Yes, I'm to meet him at the station at three, and come straight on to the church.'

Her face looked pale, but there was a brightness in the eyes and a softness about the mouth that spoke of renewed happiness.

'Mr Branbridge begged him so to stay another night that he had not the heart to refuse,' she went on. 'He is so kind, but . . . I wish he hadn't stayed.'

I was at the station at half-past two. I felt rather annoyed with John. It seemed a sort of slight to the beautiful girl who loved him, that he should come, as it were out of breath, and with the dust of travel upon him, to take her hand, which some of us would have given the best years of our life to take.

But when the three o'clock train glided in and glided out again, having brought no passengers to our little station, I was more than annoyed. There was no other train for thirty-five minutes; I calculated that, with much hurry, we might just get to the church in time for the ceremony; but, oh, what a fool to miss that first train! What other man would have done it?

The thirty-five minutes seemed a year, as I wandered round the station reading the advertisements and the time-tables and the company's bye-laws, and getting more and more angry with John Charrington. This confidence in his own power of getting everything he wanted the minute he wanted it, was leading him too far.

I hate waiting. Everyone hates waiting, but I believe I hate it more than anyone else does. The three-thirty-five was late too, of course.

I ground my pipe between my teeth and stamped with impatience as I watched the signals. Click. The signal went down. Five minutes later I flung myself into the carriage that I had brought for John.

'Drive to the church!' I said, as someone shut the door. 'Mr Charrington hasn't come by this train.'

Anxiety now replaced anger. What had become of this man? Could he have been taken suddenly ill? I had never known him have a day's illness in his life. And even so he might have telegraphed. Some awful accident must have happened to him. The thought that he had played her false never, no, not for a moment, entered my head. Yes, something terrible had happened to him, and on me lay the task of telling his bride. I almost wished the carriage would upset and break my head, so that someone else might tell her.

It was five minutes to four as we drew up at the church-yard. A double row of eager onlookers lined the path from lych-gate to porch. I sprang from the carriage and passed up between them. Our gardener had a good front place near the door. I stopped.

'Are they still waiting, Byles?' I asked, simply to gain time, for of course I knew they were, by the waiting crowd's attentive attitude.

'Waiting, sir? No, no, sir; why it must be over by now.'

'Over! Then Mr Charrington's come?'

'To the minute sir; must have missed you somehow, and I say, sir,' lowering his voice, 'I never see Mr John the least bit so afore, but my opinion is he's 'ad more than a drop; I wouldn't be going too far if I said he's been drinking pretty free. His clothes was all dusty and his face like a sheet. I tell you I didn't like the looks of him at all, and the folks inside are saying all sorts of things. You'll see, something's gone very wrong with Mr John, and he's tried liquor. He looked like a ghost, and he went in with his eyes straight before him, with never a look or a word for none of us; him that was always such a gentleman.'

I had never heard Byles make so long a speech. The crowd in the churchyard were talking in whispers, and getting ready rice and slippers to throw at the bride and bridegroom. The ringers were ready with their hands on the ropes, to ring out the merry peal as the bride and bridegroom should come out.

A murmur from the church announced them; out they came. Byles was right. John Charrington did not look himself. There was dust on his coat, his hair was disarranged. He seemed to have been in some row, for there was a black mark above his eyebrow. He was deathly pale. But his pallor was not greater than that of the bride, who might have been carved in ivory – dress, veil, orange-blossoms, face and all.

As they passed out, the ringers stooped – there were six of them – and then, on the ears expecting the gay wedding peal, came the slow tolling of the passing bell.

A thrill of horror at so foolish a jest from the ringers passed through us all. But the ringers themselves dropped the ropes and fled like rabbits out into the sunlight. The bride shuddered, and grey shadows came about her mouth, but the bridegroom led her on down the path where the people stood with the handfuls of rice; but the handfuls were never thrown, and the wedding bells never rang. In vain the ringers were urged to remedy their mistake; they protested, with many whispered expletives, that they had not rung that bell; that they would see themselves further before they'd ring anything more that day.

In a hush, like the hush in the chamber of death, the bridal pair passed into their carriage, and its door slammed behind them.

Then the tongues were loosed. A babel of anger, wonder, conjecture from the guests and the spectators.

'If I'd seen his condition, sir,' said old Foster to me as we drove off, 'I would have stretched him on the floor of the church, sir, by Heaven I would, before I'd have let him marry my daughter!'

Then he put his head out the window.

'Drive like hell,' he cried to the coachman; 'don't spare the horses.'

We passed the bride's carriage. I forebore to look at it, and old Foster turned his head away and swore.

We stood in the hall doorway, in the blazing afternoon sun, and in about half a minute we heard wheels crunching the gravel. When the carriage stopped in front of the steps, old Foster and I ran down.

'Great Heaven, the carriage is empty! And yet – '

I had the door open in a minute, and this is what I saw –

No sign of John Charrington; and of May, his wife, only a huddled heap of white satin, lying half on the floor of the carriage and half on the seat.

'I drove straight here, sir,' said the coachman, as the bride's father lifted her out, 'and I'll swear no one got out of the carriage.'

We carried her into the house in her bridal dress, and drew back her veil. I saw her face. Shall I ever forget it? White, white, and drawn with agony and horror, bearing such a look of terror as I have never seen since, except in dreams. And her hair, her radiant blonde hair, I tell you it was white like snow.

As we stood, her father and I, half mad with the horror and mystery of it, a boy came up the avenue – a telegraph boy. They brought the orange envelope to me. I tore it open.

'*John Charrington was thrown from the dog-cart on his way to the station at half-past one. Killed on the spot.* — BRANBRIDGE, Peasemarsh Place.'

And he was married to May Foster in our Parish Church at *half-past three*, in presence of half the parish!

'*I shall be married on Thursday dead or alive!*'

What had passed in that carriage on the homeward drive? No one knows – no one will ever know.

Before a week was over they laid her beside her husband in the churchyard where they had kept their love-trysts.

This is the true story of John Charrington's wedding.

THE SHADOW

This is not an artistically rounded off ghost story, and nothing is explained in it, and there seems to be no reason why any of it should have happened. But that is no reason why it should not be told. You must have noticed that all the real ghost stories you have ever come close to, are like this in these respects - no explanation, no logical coherence. Here is the story.

There were three of us and another, but she had fainted suddenly at the second extra of the Christmas dance, and had been put to bed in the dressing-room next to the room which we three shared. It had been one of those jolly, old-fashioned dances where nearly everybody stays the night, and the big country house is stretched to its utmost containing - guests harbouring on sofas, couches, settles, and even mattresses on floors. Some of the young men actually, I believe, slept on the great dining-table. We had talked of our partners, as girls will, and then the stillness of the manor house, broken only by the whisper of the wind in the cedar branches, and the scraping of their harsh fingers against our window panes, had pricked us to such a luxurious confidence in our surroundings of bright chintz and candle-flame and fire-light, that we had dared to talk of ghosts - in which, we all said, we did not believe one bit. We had told the story of the phantom coach, and the horribly strange bed, and the lady in the sacque, and the house in Berkeley Square.

We none of us believed in ghosts, but my heart, at least, seemed to leap to my throat and choke me there, when a tap came to our door - a tap faint, not to be mistaken.

'Who's there?' said the youngest of us, craning a lean neck towards the door. It opened slowly, and I give you my word the instant of suspense that followed is still reckoned among my life's least confident moments. Almost at once the door opened fully, and Miss Eastwich, my aunt's housekeeper, companion and general stand-by, looked in on us.

We all said 'come in,' but she stood there. She was, at all normal hours, the most silent woman I have ever known. She stood and looked at us, and shivered a little. So did we, for in those days corridors were not warmed by hot-water pipes, and the air from the door was keen.

'I saw your light,' she said at last, 'and I thought it was late for you to be up – after all this gaiety. I thought perhaps – ' her glance turned towards the door of the dressing-room.

'No,' I said, 'she's fast asleep.' I should have added a good-night, but the youngest of us forestalled my speech. She did not know Miss Eastwich as we others did; did not know how her persistent silence had built a wall round her – a wall that no one dared to break down with the commonplaces of talk, or the littlenesses of mere human relationship. Miss Eastwich's silence had taught us to treat her as a machine; and as other than a machine we never dreamed of treating her. But the youngest of us had seen Miss Eastwich for the first time that day. She was young, crude, ill-balanced, subject to blind, calf-like impulses. She was also the heiress of a rich tallow-chandler, but that has nothing to do with this part of the story. She jumped up from the hearth-rug, her unsuitably rich silk lace-trimmed dressing-gown falling back from her thin collar-bones, and ran to the door and put an arm round Miss Eastwich's prim, lisse-encircled neck. I gasped. I should as soon have dared to embrace Cleopatra's Needle. 'Come in,' said the youngest of us – 'come in and get warm. There's lots of cocoa left.' She drew Miss Eastwich in and shut the door.

The vivid light of pleasure in the housekeeper's pale eyes went through my heart like a knife. It would have been so easy to put an arm round her neck, if one had only thought she wanted an arm there. But it was not I who had thought that – and indeed, my arm might not have brought the light evoked by the thin arm of the youngest of us.

'Now,' the youngest went on eagerly, 'you shall have the very biggest, nicest chair, and the cocoa-pot's here on the hob as hot as hot – and we've all been telling ghost stories, only we don't believe in them a bit; and when you get warm you ought to tell one too.'

Miss Eastwich – that model of decorum and decently done duties, tell a ghost story!

'You're sure I'm not in your way,' Miss Eastwich said, stretching her hands to the blaze. I wondered whether housekeepers have fires in their rooms even at Christmas time. 'Not a bit' – I said it, and I hope I said it as warmly as I felt it. 'I – Miss Eastwich – I'd have asked you to come in other times – only I didn't think you'd care for girls' chatter.'

The third girl, who was really of no account, and that's why I have not said anything about her before, poured cocoa for our guest. I put my fleecy Madeira shawl round her shoulders. I could not think of anything else to do for her, and I found myself wishing desperately to do something. The smiles she gave us were quite pretty. People can smile prettily at forty or fifty, or even later, though girls don't realise this. It occurred to me, and this was another knife-thrust, that I had never seen Miss Eastwich smile – a real smile, before. The pale smiles of dutiful acquiescence were not of the same blood as this dimpling, happy, transfiguring look.

'This is very pleasant,' she said, and it seemed to me that I had never before heard her real voice. It did not please me to think that at the cost of cocoa, a fire, and my arm round her neck, I might have heard this new voice any time these six years.

'We've been telling ghost stories,' I said. 'The worst of it is, we don't believe in ghosts. No one one knows has ever seen one.'

'It's always what somebody told somebody, who told somebody you know,' said the youngest of us, 'and you can't believe that, can you?'

'What the soldier said, is not evidence,' said Miss Eastwich. Will it be believed that the little Dickens quotation pierced one more keenly than the new smile or the new voice?

'And all the ghost stories are so beautifully rounded off – a murder committed on the spot – or a hidden treasure, or a warning – I think that makes them harder to believe. The most horrid ghost-story I ever heard was one that was quite silly.'

'Tell it.'

'I can't – it doesn't sound anything to tell. Miss Eastwich ought to tell one.'

'Oh do,' said the youngest of us, and her salt cellars loomed dark, as she stretched her neck eagerly and laid an entreating arm on our guest's knee.

'The only thing that I ever knew of was – was hearsay,' she said slowly, 'till just the end.'

I knew she would tell her story, and I knew she had never before told it, and I knew she was only telling it now because she was proud, and this seemed the only way to pay for the fire and the cocoa, and the laying of that arm round her neck.

'Don't tell it,' I said suddenly. 'I know you'd rather not.'

'I daresay it would bore you,' she said meekly, and the youngest of us, who, after all, did not understand everything, glared resentfully at me.

'We should just *love* it,' she said. '*Do* tell us. Never mind if it isn't a real, proper, fixed up story. I'm certain anything *you* think ghostly would be quite too beautifully horrid for anything.'

Miss Eastwich finished her cocoa and reached up to set the cup on the mantelpiece.

'It can't do any harm,' she said half to herself, 'they

don't believe in ghosts, and it wasn't exactly a ghost either. And they're all over twenty – they're not babies.'

There was a breathing time of hush and expectancy. The fire crackled and the gas suddenly glared higher because the billiard lights had been put out. We heard the steps and voices of the men going along the corridors.

'It is really hardly worth telling,' Miss Eastwich said doubtfully, shading her faded face from the fire with her thin hand.

We all said 'Go on – oh, go on – do!'

'Well,' she said, 'twenty years ago – and more than that – I had two friends, and I loved them more than anything in the world. And they married each other –'

She paused, and I knew just in what way she had loved each of them. The youngest of us said –

'How awfully nice for you. Do go on.'

She patted the youngest's shoulder, and I was glad that I had understood, and that the youngest of all hadn't. She went on.

'Well, after they were married, I did not see much of them for a year or two; and then he wrote and asked me to come and stay, because his wife was ill, and I should cheer her up, and cheer him up as well; for it was a gloomy house, and he himself was growing gloomy too.'

I knew, as she spoke, that she had every line of that letter by heart.

'Well, I went. The address was in Lee, near London; in those days there were streets and streets of new villa-houses growing up round old brick mansions standing in their own grounds, with red walls round, you know, and a sort of flavour of coaching days, and post chaises, and Blackheath highwaymen about them. He had said the house was gloomy, and it was called '*The Firs*,' and I imagined my cab going through a dark, winding shrubbery, and drawing up in front of one of these sedate, old, square houses. Instead, we drew up in front of a large, smart villa, with iron railings, gay encaustic tiles leading from the iron gate to the stained-glass-panelled door, and for shrubbery only a few stunted cypresses and aucubas in the tiny front garden. But inside it was all warm and welcoming. He met me at the door.'

She was gazing into the fire, and I knew she had forgotten us. But the youngest girl of all still thought it was to us she was telling her story.

'He met me at the door,' she said again, 'and thanked me for coming, and asked me to forgive the past.'

'What past?' said the high priestess of the *inàpropos*, the youngest of all.

'Oh – I suppose he meant because they hadn't invited me before, or something,' said Miss Eastwich worriedly, 'but it's a very dull story, I find, after all, and –'

'Do go on,' I said – then I kicked the youngest of us, and got up to rearrange Miss Eastwich's shawl, and said in blatant dumb show, over the shawled shoulder: 'Shut up, you little idiot –'

After another silence, the housekeeper's new voice went on.

'They were very glad to see me, and I was very glad to be there. You girls, now, have such troops of friends, but these two were all I had – all I had ever had. Mabel wasn't exactly ill, only weak and excitable. I thought he seemed more ill than she did. She went to bed early and before she went, she asked me to keep him company through his last pipe, so we went into the dining room and sat in the two armchairs on each side of the fireplace. They were covered with green leather I remember. There were bronze groups of horses and a black marble clock on the mantelpiece – all wedding presents. He poured out some whisky for himself, but he hardly touched it. He sat looking into the fire. At last I said:–

' "What's wrong? Mabel looks as well as you could expect."

'He said, "Yes – but I don't know from one day to another that she won't begin to notice something wrong.

That's why I wanted you to come. You were always so sensible and strong-minded, and Mabel's like a little bird on a flower."

'I said yes, of course, and waited for him to go on. I thought he must be in debt, or in trouble of some sort. So I just waited. Presently he said:

'"Margaret, this is a very peculiar house –" he always called me Margaret. You see we'd been such old friends. I told him I thought the house was very pretty, and fresh, and homelike – only a little too new – but that fault would mend with time. He said:–

'"It *is* new: that's just it. We're the first people who've ever lived in it. If it were an old house, Margaret, I should think it was haunted."

'I asked if he had seen anything. "No," he said "not yet."

'"Heard then?" said I.

'"No – not heard either," he said "but there's a sort of feeling: I can't describe it – I've seen nothing and I've heard nothing, but I've been so near to seeing and hearing, just near, that's all. And something follows me about – only when I turn round, there's never anything, only my shadow. And I always feel that I *shall* see the thing next minute – but I never do – not quite – it's always just not visible."

'I thought he'd been working rather hard – and tried to cheer him up by making light of all this. It was just nerves, I said. Then he said he had thought I could help him, and did I think anyone he had wronged could have laid a curse on him, and did I believe in curses. I said I didn't – and the only person anyone could have said he had wronged forgave him freely, I knew, if there was anything to forgive. So I told him this too.'

It was I, not the youngest of us, who knew the name of that person, wronged and forgiving.

'So then I said he ought to take Mabel away from the house and have a complete change. But he said No; Mabel had got everything in order, and he could never manage to get her away just now without explaining everything – "and, above all," he said, "she mustn't guess there's anything wrong. I daresay I shan't feel quite such a lunatic now you're here."

'So we said good-night.'

'Is that all the story!' said the third girl, striving to convey that even as it stood it was a good story.

'That's only the beginning,' said Miss Eastwich. 'Whenever I was alone with him he used to tell me the same thing over and over again, and at first when I began to notice things, I tried to think that it was his talk that had upset my nerves. The odd thing was that it wasn't only at night – but in broad daylight – and particularly on the stairs and passages. On the staircase the feeling used to be so awful that I have had to bite my lips till they bled to keep myself from running upstairs at full speed. Only I knew if I did I should go mad at the top. There was always something behind me - exactly as he had said - something that one could just not see. And a sound that one could just not hear. There was a long corridor at the top of the house. I have sometimes almost seen something – you know how one sees things without looking – but if I turned round, it seemed as if the thing drooped and melted into my shadow. There was a little window at the end of the corridor.

'Downstairs there was another corridor, something like it, with a cupboard at one end and the kitchen at the other. One night I went down into the kitchen to heat some milk for Mabel. The servants had gone to bed. As I stood by the fire, waiting for the milk to boil, I glanced through the open door and along the passage. I never could keep my eyes on what I was doing in that house. The cupboard door was partly open; they used to keep empty boxes and things in it. And, as I looked, I knew that now it was not going to be "almost" any more. Yet I said, "Mabel?" - not because I thought it could be Mabel who was crouching down there, half in and half out of the cupboard. The thing was grey at first, and then it was black. And when I whispered, "Mabel," it seemed to sink down till it lay like a pool of ink on the floor, and then its edges drew in, and it seemed to flow, like ink when you tilt up the paper you have spilt it on; and it flowed into the cupboard till it was all gathered into the shadow there. I saw it go quite plainly. The gas was full on in the kitchen. I screamed aloud, but even then, I'm thankful to say, I had enough sense to upset the boiling milk, so that when he came downstairs three steps at a time, I had the excuse for my scream of a scalded hand. The explanation satisfied Mabel, but next night he said:

' "Why didn't you tell me? It was that cupboard. All the horror of the house comes out of that. Tell me – have you seen anything yet? Or is it only the nearly seeing and nearly hearing still?"

'I said, "You must tell me first what you've seen." He told me, and his eyes wandered, as he spoke, to the shadows by the curtains, and I turned up all three gas lights, and lit the candles on the mantelpiece. Then we looked at each other and said we were both mad, and thanked God that Mabel at least was sane. For what he had seen was what I had seen.

'After that I hated to be alone with a shadow, because at any moment I might see something that would crouch, and sink, and lie like a black pool, and then slowly draw itself into the shadow that was nearest. Often that shadow was my own. The thing came first at night, but afterwards there was no hour safe from it. I saw it at dawn and at noon, in the dusk and in the firelight, and always it crouched and sank, and was a pool that flowed into some shadow and became part of it. And always I saw it with a straining of the eyes – a pricking and aching. It seemed as though I could only just see it, as if my sight, to see it, had to be strained to the uttermost. And still the sound was in the house – the sound that I could just not hear. At last,

one morning early, I did hear it. It was close behind me, and it was only a sigh. It was worse than the thing that crept into the shadows.

'I don't know how I bore it. I couldn't have borne it, if I hadn't been so fond of them both. But I knew in my heart that, if he had no one to whom he could speak openly, he would go mad, or tell Mabel. His was not a very strong character; very sweet, and kind, and gentle, but not strong. He was always easily led. So I stayed on and bore up, and we were very cheerful, and made little jokes, and tried to be amusing when Mabel was with us. But when we were alone, we did not try to be amusing. And sometimes a day or two would go by without our seeing or hearing anything, and we should perhaps have fancied that we had fancied what we had seen and heard – only there was always the feeling of there being something about the house, that one could just not hear and not see. Sometimes we used to try not to talk about it, but generally we talked of nothing else at all. And the weeks went by, and Mabel's baby was born. The nurse and the doctor said that both mother and child were doing well. He and I sat late in the dining-room that night. We had neither of us seen or heard anything for three days; our anxiety about Mabel was lessened. We talked of the future – it seemed then so much brighter than the past. We arranged that, the moment she was fit to be moved, he should take her away to the sea, and I should superintend the moving of their furniture into the new house he had already chosen. He was gayer than I had seen him since his marriage – almost like his old self. When I said good-night to him, he said a lot of things about my having been a comfort to them both. I hadn't done anything much, of course, but still I am glad he said them.

'Then I went upstairs, almost for the first time without that feeling of something following me. I listened at Mabel's door. Everything was quiet. I went on towards my own room, and in an instant I felt that there *was* something behind me. I turned. It was crouching there; it sank, and the black fluidness of it seemed to be sucked under the door of Mabel's room.

'I went back. I opened the door a listening inch. All was still. And then I heard a sigh close behind me. I opened the door and went in. The nurse and the baby were asleep. Mabel was asleep too; she looked so pretty, like a tired child – the baby was cuddled up into one of her arms with its tiny head against her side. I prayed then that Mabel might never know the terrors that he and I had known. That those little ears might never hear any but pretty sounds, those clear eyes never see any but pretty sights. I did not dare to pray for a long time after that. Because my prayer was answered. She never saw, never heard anything more in this world. And now I could do nothing more for him or for her.

'When they had put her in her coffin, I lighted wax candles round her, and laid the horrible white flowers that people will send near her, and then I saw he had followed me. I took his hand to lead him away.

'At the door we both turned. It seemed to us that we heard a sigh. He would have sprung to her side, in I don't know what mad, glad hope. But in that instant we both saw it. Between us and the coffin, first grey, then black, it crouched an instant, then sank and liquefied, and was gathered together and drawn till it ran into the nearest shadow. And the nearest shadow was the shadow of Mabel's coffin. I left the next day. His mother came. She had never liked me.'

Miss Eastwich paused. I think she had quite forgotten us.

'Didn't you see him again?' asked the youngest of us all.

'Only once,' Miss Eastwich answered, 'and something black crouched then between him and me. But it was only his second wife, crying beside his coffin. It's not a cheerful story is it? And it doesn't lead anywhere. I've never told anyone else. I think it was seeing his daughter that brought it all back.'

She looked towards the dressing-room door.

'Mabel's baby?'

'Yes – and exactly like Mabel, only with his eyes.'

The youngest of all had Miss Eastwich's hands, and was petting them.

Suddenly the woman wrenched her hands away, and stood at her gaunt height, her hands clenched, eyes straining. She was looking at something that we could not see, and I know what the man in the Bible meant when he said: 'The hair of my flesh stood up.'

What she saw seemed not quite to reach the height of the dressing-room door handle. Her eyes followed it down, down – widening and widening. Mine followed them – all the nerves of them seemed strained to the uttermost – and I almost saw – or did I quite see? I can't be certain. But we all heard the long-drawn, quivering sigh. And to each of us it seemed to be breathed just behind us.

It was I who caught up the candle – it dripped all over my trembling hand – and was dragged by Miss Eastwich to the girl who had fainted during the second extra. But it was the youngest of all whose lean arms were round the housekeeper when we turned away, and that have been round her many a time since, in the new home where she keeps house for the youngest of us.

The doctor who came in the morning said that Mabel's daughter had died of heart disease – which she had inherited from her mother. It was that that had made her faint during the second extra. But I have sometimes wondered whether she may not have inherited something from her father. I have never been able to forget the look on her dead face.

THE FIVE SENSES

Professor Boyd Thompson's services to the cause of science are usually spoken of as inestimable, and so indeed they probably are, since in science, as in the rest of life, one thing leads to another, and you never know where anything is going to stop. At any rate, inestimable or not, they are world-renowned, and he with them. The discoveries which he gave to his time are a matter of common knowledge among biological experts, and the sudden ending of his experimental activities caused a few days' wonder in even lay circles. Quite unintelligent people told each other that it seemed a pity, and persons on omnibuses exchanged commonplaces starred with his name.

But the real meaning and cause of that ending have been studiously hidden, as well as the events which immediately preceded it. A veil has been drawn over all the things that people would have liked to know, and it is only now that circumstances so arrange themselves as to make it possible to tell the whole story. I propose to avail myself of this possibility.

It will serve no purpose for me to explain how the necessary knowledge came into my possession; but I will say that the story was only in part pieced together by me. Another hand is responsible for much of the detail, and for a certain occasional emotionalism which is, I believe, wholly foreign to my own style. In my original statement of the following facts I dealt fully, as I am, I may say without immodesty, qualified to do, with all the scientific points of the narrative. But these details were judged, unwisely as I think, to be needless to the expert, and unintelligible to the ordinary reader, and have therefore been struck out; the merest hints being left as necessary links in the story. This appears to me to destroy most of its interest, but I admit that the elisions are perhaps justified. I have no desire to assist or encourage callow students in such experiments as those by which Professor Boyd Thompson brought his scientific career to an end.

Incredible as it may appear, Professor Boyd Thompson was once a little boy who wore white embroidered frocks and blue sashes; in that state he caught flies and pulled off their wings to find out how they flew. He did not find out, and Lucilla, his little girl-cousin, also in white frocks, cried over the dead, dismembered flies, and buried them in little paper coffins. Later, he wore a holland blouse with a belt of leather, and watched the development of tadpoles in a tin bath in the stable yard. A microscope was, on his eighth birthday, presented to him by an affluent uncle. The uncle showed him how to surprise the secrets of a drop of pond water, which, limpid to the eye, confessed under the microscope to a whole cosmogony of strenuous and undesirable careers. At the age of ten, Arthur Boyd Thompson was sent to a private school, its Headmaster an acolyte of Science, who esteemed himself to be a high priest of Huxley and Tyndal, a devotee of Darwin. Thence to the choice of medicine as a profession was, when the choice was insisted on by the elder Boyd Thompson, a short, plain step. Inorganic chemistry failed to charm, and under the cloak of Medicine and Surgery the growing fever of scientific curiosity could be sated on bodies other than the cloak-wearer's. He became a medical student and an enthusiast for vivisection.

The bow of Apollo was not always bent. In a rest-interval, the summer vacation, to be exact, he met again the cousin—second, once removed—Lucilla, and loved her. They were betrothed. It was a long, bright summer full of sunshine, garden-parties, picnics, archery—a decaying amusement—and croquet, then coming to its own. He exulted in the distinction already crescent in his career but some half-formed, wholly-unconscious desire to shine with increased lustre in the eyes of the beloved, caused him to invite, for the holidays' ultimate week, a fellow student, one who knew and could testify to the quality of the laurels already encircling the head of the young scientist. The friend came, testified, and in a vibrating interview under the lime-trees of Lucilla's people's garden, Mr Boyd Thompson learned that Lucilla never could, never would love or marry a vivisectionist.

The moon hung low and yellow in the spacious calm of the sky; the hour was propitious, the lovers fond. Mr Boyd Thompson vowed that his scientific research should henceforth deal wholly with departments into which the emotions of the non-scientific cannot enter. He went back to London, and within the week bought four dozen frogs, twelve guinea-pigs, five cats, and a spaniel. His scientific aspirations met his love-longings, and did not fight them. You cannot fight beings of another world. He took part in a debate on blood pressure, which created some little stir in medical circles, spoke eloquently, and distinction surrounded him with a halo.

He wrote to Lucilla three times a week, took his degree, and published that celebrated paper of his which set the whole scientific world by the ears, 'The Action of Choline on the Nervous System,' I think its name was.

Lucilla surreptitiously subscribed to a press-cutting agency for all snippets of print relating to her lover. Three weeks after the publication of that paper, which really was the beginning of Professor Boyd Thompson's fame, she wrote to him from her home in Kent.

'Arthur, you have been doing it again. You know how I love you, and I believe you love me; but you must choose between loving me and torturing dumb animals. If you don't choose right, then it's good-bye, and God forgive you.

Your poor Lucilla, who loved you very dearly.'

He read the letter, and the human heart in him winced and whined. Yet not so deeply now, nor so loudly, but that he bethought himself to seek out a friend and pupil, who

would watch certain experiments, attend to the cutting of
certain sections, before he started for Tenterden, where
she lived. There was no station at Tenterden in those days,
but a twelve mile walk did not dismay him.

Lucilla's home was one of those houses of brave proportions and an inalienable bourgeois stateliness, which stand
back a little from the noble High Street of that most
beautiful of Kentish towns. He came there pleasantly ex-
ercised, his boots dusty, and his throat dry, and stood on
the snowy doorstep, beneath the Jacobean lintel. He
looked down the wide, beautiful street, raised eyebrows
and shrugged uneasy shoulders within his professional
frock-coat.

'It's all so difficult,' he said to himself.

Lucilla received him in a drawing-room scented with
last year's rose leaves, and fresh with chintz that had been
washed a dozen times. She stood, very pale and frail; her
blonde hair was not teased into fluffiness, and rounded
over the chignon of the period, but banded Madonna-
wise, crowning her with heavy burnished plaits. Her gown
was of white muslin, and round her neck black velvet
passed, supporting a gold locket. He knew whose picture
it held. The loose bell sleeves fell away from the slender
arms with little black velvet bracelets, and she leaned one
hand on a chiffonier of carved rosewood, on whose marble
top stood, under a glass case, a Chinese pagoda, carved in
ivory, and two Bohemian glass vases with medallions representing young women nursing pigeons. There were
white curtains of darned net, in the fire-place white rav-
elled muslin spread a cascade brightened with threads of
tinsel. A canary sang in a green cage, wainscotted with
yellow tarlatan, and two red rosebuds stood in lank speci-
men glasses on the mantelpiece.

Every article of furniture in the room spoke eloquently
of the sheltered life, the iron obstinacy of the well-
brought-up.

It was a scene that invaded his mental vision many a

time, in the laboratory, in the lecture-room. It symbolised many things, all dear, and all impossible.

They talked awkwardly, miserably. And always it came round to this same thing.

'But you don't mean it,' he said, and at last came close to her.

'I do mean it,' she said, very white, very trembling, very determined.

'But it's my life,' he pleaded, 'it's the life of thousands. You don't understand.'

'I understand that dogs are tortured. I can't bear it.'

He caught at her hand.

'Don't,' she said. 'When I think what that hand does!'

'Dearest,' he said very earnestly, 'which is the more important, a dog or a human being?'

'They're all God's creatures,' she flashed, unorthodoxly orthodox. 'They're all God's creatures,' with much more that he heard, and pitied, and smiled at miserably in his heart.

'You don't understand,' he kept saying, stemming the flood of her rhetorical pleadings. 'Spencer Wells alone has found out wonderful things, just with experiments on rabbits.'

'Don't tell me,' she said, 'I don't want to hear.'

The conventions of their day forbade that he should tell her anything plainly. He took refuge in generalities. 'Spencer Wells, that operation he perfected, it's restored thousands of women to their husbands – saved thousands of women for their children.'

'I don't care what he's done – it's wrong if it's done in that way.'

It was on that day that they parted, after more than an hour and more than two, of mutual misunderstood reiteration. He, she said, was brutal. And besides it was plain that he did not love her. To him, she seemed unreasonable, narrow, prejudiced, blind to the high ideals of the new science.

'Then it's goodbye,' he said at last. 'If I gave way, you'd
only despise me. Because I should despise myself. It's no
good. Goodbye, dear.'

'Goodbye,' she said. 'I know I'm right. You'll know I
am, some day.'

'Never,' he answered, more moved and in a more dif-
fused sense than he had ever believed he could be. 'I can't
set my pleasure in you against the good of the whole
world.'

'If that's all you think of me,' she said, and her silk and
her muslin whirled from the room.

He walked back to Staplehurst, thrilled with the conflict. The thrill died down, went out, and left as ashes a
cold resolve.

That was the end of Mr Boyd Thompson's engagement.

It was quite by accident that he made his greatest discovery. There are those who hold that all great discoveries
are accident – or Providence. The terms are in this connec-
tion, interchangeable. He plunged into work to wash away
the traces of his soul's wounds, as a man plunges into water
to wash off red blood. And he swam there, perhaps, a little
blindly. The injection with which he treated that white
rabbit was not compounded of the drugs he had intended
to use. He could not lay his hand on the thing he wanted,
and in that sort of frenzy of experiment, to which no
scientific investigator is wholly a stranger, he cast about
for a new idea. The thing that came to his hand was a drug
that he had never in his normal mind intended to use – an
unaccredited, wild, magic, medicine obtained by a mis-
sionary from some savage South Sea tribe and brought
home as an example of the ignorance of the heathen.

And it worked a miracle.

He had been fighting his way through the unbending
opposition of known facts, he had been struggling in the
shadows, and this discovery was like the blinding light that
meets a man's eyes when his pickaxe knocks a hole in a

dark cave, and he finds himself face to face with the sun. The effect was undoubted. Now it behoved him to make sure of the cause, to eliminate all those other factors to which that effect might have been due. He experimented cautiously, slowly. These things take years, and the years he did not grudge. He was never tired, never impatient; the slightest variations, the least indications, were eagerly observed, faithfully recorded.

His whole soul was in his work, Lucilla was the one beautiful memory of his life. But she was a memory. The reality was this discovery, the accident, the Providence.

Day followed day, all alike, and yet each taking, almost unperceived, one little step forward; or stumbling into sudden sloughs, those losses and lapses that take days and weeks to retrieve. He was Professor, and his hair was grey at the temples before his achievement rose before him, beautiful, inevitable, austere in its completed splendour, as before the triumphant artist rises the finished work of his art.

He had found out one of the secrets with which Nature has crammed her dark hiding-places. He had discovered the hidden possibilities of sensation. In plain English, his researches had led him thus far: he had found – by accident or by Providence – the way to intensify sensation. Vaguely, incredulously, he had perceived his discovery; the rabbits and guinea-pigs had demonstrated it plainly enough. Then there was a night when he became aware that those results must be checked by something else. He must work out in marble the form he had worked out in clay. He knew that by this drug, which had, so to speak, thrust itself upon him, he could intensify the five senses of any of the inferior animals. Could he intensify those senses in man? If so, worlds beyond the grasp of his tired mind opened themselves before him. If so, he would have achieved a discovery, made a contribution to the science he had loved so well and followed at such a cost, a discovery equal to any that any man had ever made.

Ferrier, and Leo, and Horsley; those he would outshine. Galileo, Newton, Harvey; he would rank with these.

Could he find a human rabbit to submit to the test?

The soul of the man Lucilla had loved, turned and revolted. No: he had experimented on guinea-pigs and rabbits, but when it came to experimenting on men, there was only one man on whom he chose to use his new-found powers. Himself.

At least she would not have it to say that he was a coward, or unfair, when it came to the point of what a man could do and dare, could suffer and endure.

His big laboratory was silent and deserted. His assistants were gone, his private pupils dispersed. He was alone with the tools of his trade. Shelf on shelf of smooth stoppered bottles, drugs and stains, the long bench gleaming with beakers, test tubes, and the glass mansions of costly apparatus. In the shadows at the far end of the room, where the last going assistant had turned off the electric lights, strange shapes lurked, wicker-covered carboys, kinographs, galvanometers, the faintly threatening aspect of delicate complex machines all wires and coils and springs, the gaunt form of the pendulum myograph, and certain well-worn tables and copper troughs, for which the moment had no use.

He knew that this drug with others, diversely compounded and applied, produced in animals an abnormal intensification of the senses; that it increased – nay, as it were magnified a thousandfold, the hearing, the sight, the touch – and he was almost sure the senses of taste and smell. But of the extent of the increase he could form no exact estimate.

Should he tonight put himself in the position of one able to speak on these points with authority? Or should he go to the Royal Society's meeting, and hear that ass Netherby maunder yet once again about the Secretion of Lymph?

He pulled out his notebook and laid it open on the bench. He went to the locked cupboard, unfastened it with the bright key that hung instead of seal or charm at his watch-chain. He unfolded a paper and laid it on the bench where no one coming in could fail to see it. Then he took out little bottles, three, four, five, polished a graduated glass and dropped into it slow, heavy drops. A larger bottle yielded a medium in which all mingled. He hardly hesitated at all before turning up his sleeve and slipping the tiny needle into his arm. He pressed the end of the syringe. The injection was made.

Its effect, though not immediate, was sudden. He had to close his eyes, staggered indeed and was glad of the stool near him; for the drug coursed through him as a hunt in full cry might sweep over untrodden plains. Then suddenly everything seemed to settle; he was no longer the helpless scene of incredible meetings, but Professor Boyd Thompson who had injected a mixture of certain drugs, and was experiencing their effect.

His fingers, still holding the glass syringe, sent swift messages to his brain. When he looked down at his fingers, he saw that what they grasped was the smooth, slender tube of clear glass. What he felt that they held was a tremendous cylinder, rough to the touch. He wondered, even at the moment, why, if his sense of touch were indeed magnified to this degree, everything did not appear enormous – his ring, his collar. He examined the new phenomenon with cold care. It seemed that only that was enlarged on which his attention, his mind, was fixed. He kept his hand on the glass syringe, and thought of his ring, got his mind away from the tube, back again in time to feel it small between his fingers, grow, increase, and become big once more.

'So *that's* a success,' he said, and saw himself lay the thing down. It lay just in front of the rack of test tubes, to the eye just that little glass cylinder. To the touch it was like a water-pipe on a house side, and the test tubes, when he touched them, like the pipes of a great organ.

'Success,' he said again, and mixed the antidote. For he

had found the antidote in one of those flashes of intuition, imagination, genius, that light the ways of science as stars light the way of a ship in dark waters. The action of the antidote was enough for one night. He locked the cupboard, and, after all, was glad to listen to the maunderings of Netherby. It had been lonely there, in the atmosphere of complete success.

One by one, day by day, he tested the action of his drugs on his other senses. Without being technical, I had perhaps better explain that the compelling drug was, in each case, one and the same. Its action was directed to this set of nerves or that by means of the other drugs mixed with it. I trust this is clear?

The sense of smell was tested, and its laboratory, with its mingled odours, became abominable to him. Hardly could he stay himself from rushing forth into the outer air, to wash his nostrils in the clear coolness of Hampstead Heath. The sense of taste gave him, magnified a thousand times, the flavour of his after-dinner coffee, and other tastes, distasteful almost beyond the bearing point.

'But success,' he said, rinsing his mouth at the laboratory sink after the drinking of the antidote, 'all along the line, success.'

Then he tested the action of his discovery on the sense of hearing. And the sound of London came like the roar of a giant, yet when he fixed his attention on the movements of a fly, all other sounds ceased, and he heard the sound of the fly's feet on the shelf when it walked. Thus, in turn, he heard the creak of boards expanding in the heat, the movement of the glass stoppers that kept imprisoned in their proper bottles the giants of acid and alkali.

'Success!' he cried aloud, and his voice sounded in his ears like the shout of a monster overcoming primeval forces. 'Success! success!'

There remained only the eyes, and here, strangely enough, the Professor hesitated, faint with a sudden heart-sickness. Following all intensification there must be reaction. What if the reaction exceeded that from which it reacted, what if the wave of tremendous sight, stemmed by the antidote ebbing, left him blind? But the spirit of the explorer in science is the spirit that explores African rivers, and sails amid white bergs to seek the undiscovered Pole.

He held the syringe with a firm hand, made the required puncture, and braced himself for the result. His eyes seemed to swell to great globes, to dwindle to microscopic globules, to swim in a flood of fire, to shrivel high and dry on a beach of hot sand. Then he saw, and the glass fell from his hand. For the whole of the stable earth seemed to be suddenly set in movement, even the air grew thick with vast overlapping shapeless shapes. He opined later that these were the microbes and bacilli that cover and fill all things, in this world that looks so clean and bright.

Concentrating his vision, he saw in the one day's little dust on the bottles myriads of creatures, crawling and writhing, alive. The proportions of the laboratory seemed but little altered. Its large lines and forms remained practically unchanged. It was the little things that were no longer little, the invisible things that were now invisible no longer. And he felt grateful for the first time in his life, for the limits set by Nature to the powers of the human body. He had increased those powers. If he let his eyes stray idly about, as one does in the waltz for example, all was much as it used to be. But the moment he looked steadily at any one thing, it became enormous.

He closed his eyes. Success here had gone beyond his wildest dreams. Indeed he could not but feel that success, taking the bit between its teeth, had perhaps gone just the least little bit too far.

And on the next day he decided to examine the drug in all its aspects, to court the intensification of all his senses which should set him in the position of supreme power over men and things, transform him from a Professor into a demi-god.

The great question was, of course, how the five preparations of his drug would act on or against each other. Would it be intensification, or would they neutralise each other? Like all imaginative scientists, he was working with stuff perilously like the spells of magic, and certain things were not possible to be foretold. Besides, this drug came from a land of mystery and the knowledge of secrets which we call magic. He did not anticipate any increase in the danger of the experiment. Nevertheless he spent some hours in arranging and destroying papers, among others certain pages of the yellow note-book. After dinner he detained his man as, laden with the last tray, he was leaving the room.

'I may as well tell you, Parker,' the Professor said, moved by some impulse he had not expected 'that you will benefit to some extent by my will. On conditions. If any accident should cut short my life, you will at once communicate with my solicitor, whose name you will now write down.'

The model man, trained by fifteen years of close personal service, drew forth a note-book neat as the Professor's own, wrote in it neatly the address the Professor gave.

'Anything more, sir?' he asked, looking up, pencil in hand.

'No,' said the Professor, 'nothing more. Good-night, Parker.'

'Good-night, sir,' said the model man.

The next words the model man opened his lips to speak were breathed into the night tube of the nearest doctor.

'My master, Professor Boyd Thompson; could you come round at once, sir. I'm afraid it's very serious.'

It was half past six when the nearest doctor – Jones was his unimportant name – stooped over the lifeless body of the Professor.

He shook his head as he stood up and looked round the private laboratory on whose floor the body lay.

'His researches are over,' he said. 'Yes, he's dead. Been dead some hours. When did you find him?'

'I went to call my master as usual,' said Parker; 'he rises at six, summer and winter, sir. He was not in his room, and the bed had not been slept in. So I came in here, sir. It is not unusual for my master to work all night when he has been very interested in his experiments, and then he likes his coffee at six.'

'I see,' said Doctor Jones. 'Well, you'd better rouse the house and fetch his own doctor. It's heart failure, of course, but I daresay he'd like to sign the certificate himself.'

'Can nothing be done?' said Parker, much affected.

'Nothing,' said Dr Jones. 'It's the common lot. You'll have to look out for another situation.'

'Yes, sir,' said Parker; 'he told me only last night what I was to do in case of anything happening to him. I wonder if he had any idea?'

'Some premonition, perhaps,' the doctor corrected.

The funeral was a very quiet one. So the late Professor Boyd Thompson had decreed in his will. He had arranged all details. The body was to be clothed in flannel, placed in an open coffin covered only with a linen sheet, and laid in the family mausoleum, a moss-grown building in the midst of a little park which surrounded Boyd Grange, the birthplace of the Boyd Thompsons. A little property in Sussex it was. The professor sometimes went there for week-ends. He had left this property to Lucilla, with a last love-letter, in which he begged her to give his body the hospitality of the death-house, now hers with the rest of the estate. To Parker he left an annuity of two hundred pounds, on the condition that he should visit and enter the mausoleum once in every twenty-four hours for fourteen days after the funeral.

To this end the late Professor's solicitor decided that Parker had better reside at Boyd Grange for the said fortnight, and Parker, whose nerves seemed to be shaken, petitioned for company. This made easy the arrangement which the solicitor desired to make – of a witness to the carrying out by Parker of the provisions of the dead man's will. The solicitor's clerk was quite good company, and arm-in-arm with him Parker paid his first visit to the mausoleum. The little building stands in a glade of evergreen oaks. The trees are old and thick, and the narrow door is deep in shadow even on the sunniest day. Parker went to the mausoleum, peered through its square grating, but he did not go in. Instead, he listened, and his ears were full of silence.

'He's dead, right enough,' he said, with a doubtful glance at his companion.

'You ought to go in, oughtn't you?' said the solicitor's clerk.

'Go in yourself, if you like, Mr Pollack,' said Parker, suddenly angry; 'anyone who likes can go in, but it won't be me. If he was alive, it 'ud be different. I'd have done anything for *him*. But I ain't going in among all them dead and mouldering Thompsons. See? If we both say I did, it'll be just the same as me doing it.'

'So it will,' said the clerk; 'but where do I come in?'

Parker explained to him where he came in, to their mutual content.

'Right you are,' said the clerk; 'on those terms I'm fly. And if we both say you did it, we needn't come to the beastly place again,' he added, shivering and glancing over his shoulder at the door with the grating.

'No more we need,' said Parker.

Behind the bars of the narrow door lay deeper shadows than those of the ilexes outside. And in the blackest of the shadows lay a man whose every sense was intensified as though by a magic potion. For when the Professor swallowed the five variants of his great discovery, each acted as he had expected it to act. But the union of the five vehicles conveying the drug to the nerves, which served his five senses, had paralysed every muscle. His hearing, taste, touch, scent and sight were intensified a thousandfold – as they had been in the individual experiments – but the man who felt all this exaggerated increase of sensation was powerless as a cat under kurali. He could not raise a finger, stir an eyelash. More, he could not breathe, nor did his body advise him of any need of breathing. And he had lain thus immobile and felt his body slowly grow cold, had heard in thunder the voices of Parker and the doctor; had felt the enormous hands of those who made his death-toilet, had smelt intolerably the camphor and lavender that they laid round him in the narrow, black bed; had tasted the mingled flavours of the drug and its five mediums; and, in an ecstasy of magnified sensation, had made the lonely train journey which coffins make, and known himself carried into the mausoleum and left there alone. And every sense was intensified, even his sense of time, so that it seemed to him that he had lain there for many years. And the effect of the drugs showed no sign of any diminution or reaction. Why had he not left directions for the injection of the antidote? It was one of those slips which wreck campaigns, cause the discovery of hidden crimes. It was a slip, and he had made it. He had thought of death, but in all the results he had anticipated, death's semblance had found no place. Well, he had made his bed, and he must lie on it. This narrow bed, whose scent of clean oak and French polish was distinct among the musty, intolerable odours of the charnel house.

It was perhaps twenty hours that he had lain there, powerless, immobile, listening to the sounds of unexplained movements about him, when he felt with a joy, almost like delirium, a faint quivering in the eyelids.

They had closed his eyes, and till now, they had remained closed. Now, with an effort as of one who lifts a grave-stone, he raised his eyelids. They closed again quickly, for the roof of the vault, at which he gazed earnestly, was alive with monsters; spiders, earwigs, crawling beetles and flies, far too small to have been perceived by normal eyes, spread giant forms over him. He closed his eyes and shuddered. It felt like a shudder, but no one who had stood beside him could have noted any movement.

It was then that Parker came – and went.

Professor Boyd Thompson heard Parker's words, and lay listening to the thunder of Parker's retreating feet. He tried to move – to call out. But he could not. He lay there helpless, and somehow he thought of the dark end of the laboratory, where the assistant before leaving had turned out the electric lights.

He had nothing but his thoughts. He thought how he would lie there, and die there. The place was sequestered; no one passed that way. Parker had failed him, and the end was not hard to picture. He might recover all his faculties, might be able to get up, able to scream, to shout, to tear at the bars. The bars were strong, and Parker would not come again. Well, he would try to face with a decent bravery whatever had to be faced.

Time, measureless, spread round. It seemed as though someone had stopped all the clocks in the world, as though he were not in time but in eternity. Only by the waxing and waning light he knew of the night and the day.

His brain was weary with the effort to move, to speak, to cry out. He lay, informed with something like despair – or fortitude. And then Parker came again. And this time a key grated in the lock. The Professor noted with rapture that it sounded no louder than a key should sound, turned in a lock that was rusty. Nor was the voice other than he had been used to hear it, when he was man alive and Parker's master. And –

'You can go in, of course, if you wish it, Miss,' said Parker disapprovingly; 'but it's not what I should advise myself. For me it's different,' he added on a sudden instinct of self-preservation; 'I've *got* to go in. Every day for a fortnight,' he added, pitying himself.

'I will go in, thank you,' said a voice. 'Yes, give me the candle, please. And you need not wait. I will lock the door when I come out.' Thus the voice spoke. And the voice was Lucilla's.

In all his life the Professor had never feared death or its trappings. Neither its physical repulsiveness, nor the supernatural terrors which cling about it, had he either understood or tolerated. But now, in one little instant, he did understand.

He heard Lucilla come in. A light held near him shone warm and red through his closed eyelids. And he knew that he had only to unclose those eyelids to see her face bending over him. And he could unclose them. Yet he would not. He lay there, still and straight in his coffin, and life swept through him in waves of returning power. Yet he lay like death. For he said, or something in him said:

'She believes me dead. If I open my eyes it will be like a dead man looking at her. If I move it will be a dead man moving under her eyes. People have gone mad for less. Lie still, lie still,' he told himself; 'take any risks yourself. There must be none for her.'

She had taken the candle away, set it down somewhere at a distance, and now she was kneeling beside him and her hand was under his head. He knew he could raise his arm and clasp her – and Parker would come back perhaps, when she did not return to the house, come back to find a man in grave-clothes, clasping a mad woman. He lay still. Then her kisses and tears fell on his face, and she murmured broken words of love and longing. But he lay still. At any cost he must lie still. Even at the cost of his own sanity, his own life. And the warmth of her hand under his head, her face against his, her kisses, her tears, set his blood flowing evenly and strongly. Her other arm lay on his breast, softly pressing over his heart. He would not move. He would be strong. If he were to be saved, it must be by some other way, not this.

Suddenly tears and kisses ceased; her every breath seemed to have stopped with these. She had drawn away from him. She spoke. Her voice came from above him. She was standing up.

'Arthur!' she said, 'Arthur!' Then he opened his eyes, the narrowest chink. But he could not see her. Only he knew she was moving towards the door. There had been a new quality in her tone, a thrill of fear, or hope was it? or at least of uncertainty? Should he move; should he speak? He dared not. He knew too well the fear that the normal human being has of death and the grave, the fear transcending love, transcending reason. Her voice was further away now. She was by the door. She was leaving him. If he let her go, it was an end of hope for him. If he did not let her go, an end, perhaps, of reason, for her. No.

'Arthur,' she said, 'I don't believe . . . I believe you can hear me. I'm going to get a doctor. If you *can* speak, speak to me.'

Her speaking ended, cut off short as a cord is cut by a knife. He did not speak. He lay in a conscious, forced rigidity.

'Speak if you can,' she implored, 'just one word!'

Then he said, very faintly, very distinctly, in a voice that seemed to come from a great way off, 'Lucilla!'

And at the word she screamed aloud, pitifully, and leapt for the entrance; and he heard the rustle of her cape in the narrow door. Then he opened his eyes wide, and raised himself on his elbow. Very weak he was, and trembling exceedingly. To his ears her scream held the note of madness. Vainly he had refrained. Selfishly he had yielded. The cold hand of a mortal faintness clutched at his heart.

'I don't want to live now,' he told himself, and fell back in the straight bed.

Her arms were round him.

'I'm going to get help,' she said, her lips to his ear; 'brandy and things. Only I came back. I didn't want you to think I was frightened. Oh, my dear! thank God, thank God!' He felt her kisses even through the swooning mist that swirled about him. Had she really fled in terror? He never knew. He knew that she had come back to him.

That is the real, true, and authentic narrative of the events which caused Professor Boyd Thompson to abandon a brilliant career, to promise anything that Lucilla might demand, and to devote himself entirely to a gentlemanly and unprofitable farming, and to his wife. From the point of view of the scientific world it is a sad ending to much promise, but at any rate there are two happy people hand in hand at the story's ending.

There is no doubt that for several years Professor Boyd Thompson had had enough of science, and, by a natural revulsion, flung himself into the full tide of commonplace sentiment. But genius, like youth, cannot be denied. And I, for one, am doubtful whether the Professor's renunciation of research will be a lasting one. Already I have heard whispers of a laboratory which is being built on to the house, beyond the billiard-room.

But I am inclined to believe the rumours which assert that, for the future, his research will take the form of extending paths already well trodden; that he will refrain from experiments with unknown drugs, and those dreadful researches which tend to merge the chemist and biologist in the alchemist and the magician. And he certainly does not intend to experiment further on the nerves of any living thing, even his own. The Professor had already done enough work to make the reputation of half a dozen ordinary scientists. He may be pardoned if he rests on his laurels, entwining them, to some extent, with roses.

The bottle containing the drug from the South Seas was knocked down on the day of his death and swept up in bits by the laboratory boy. It is a curious fact that the Professor has wholly forgotten the formulae of his great discovery, the notes of which he destroyed just before his experiment which so nearly was his last. This is a great satisfaction to his wife, and possibly to the Professor. But of this I cannot be sure; the scientific spirit survives much.

To the unscientific reader the strangest part of this story will perhaps be the fact that Parker is still with his old master, a wonderful example of the perfect butler. Professor Boyd Thompson was able to forgive Parker because he understood him. And he learned to understand Parker in those moments of agony, when his keen intellect and his awakened heart taught him, through his love for Lucilla, the depth of that gulf of fear which lies between the quick and the dead.

THE THREE DRUGS

I

Roger Wroxham looked round his studio before he blew
out the candle, and wondered whether, perhaps, he looked
for the last time. It was large and empty, yet his trouble
had filled it, and, pressing against him in the prison of
those four walls, forced him out into the world, where
lights and voices and the presence of other men should
give him room to draw back, to set a space between it and
him, to decide whether he would ever face it again – he
and it alone together. The nature of his trouble is not
germane to this story. There was a woman in it, of course,
and money, and a friend, and regrets and embarrass-
ments—and all of these reached out tendrils that wove and
interwove till they made a puzzle-problem of which heart
and brain were now weary. It was as though his life de-
pended on his deciphering the straggling characters traced
by some spider who, having fallen into the ink-well, had
dragged clogged legs in a black zig-zag across his map of
the world.

He blew out the candle and went quietly downstairs. It
was nine at night, a soft night of May in Paris. Where
should he go? He thought of the Seine, and took – an
omnibus. The chestnut trees of the boulevards brushed
against the sides of the one that he boarded blindly in the
first light street. He did not know where the omnibus was
going. It did not matter. When at last it stopped he got off,
and so strange was the place to him that for an instant it
almost seemed as though the trouble itself had been left
behind. He did not feel it in the length of three or four
streets that he traversed slowly. But in the open space, very
light and lively, where he recognised the Taverne de Paris

and knew himself in Montmartre, the trouble set its teeth in his heart again, and he broke away from the lamps and the talk to struggle with it in the dark quiet streets beyond.

A man braced for such a fight has little thought to spare for the detail of his surroundings. The next thing that Wroxham knew of the outside world was the fact that he had known for some time that he was not alone in the street. There was someone on the other side of the road keeping pace with him – yes, certainly keeping pace, for, as he slackened his own, the feet on the other pavement also went more slowly. And now they were four feet, not two. Where had the other man sprung from? He had not been there a moment ago. And now, from an archway a little ahead of him, a third man came.

Wroxham stopped. Then three men converged upon him, and, like a sudden magic-lantern picture on a sheet prepared, there came to him all that he had heard and read of Montmartre – dark archways, knives, Apaches, and men who went away from homes where they were beloved and never again returned. He, too – well, if he never returned again, it would be quicker than the Seine, and, in the event of ultramundane possibilities, safer.

He stood still and laughed in the face of the man who first reached him.

'Well, my friend?' said he, and at that the other two drew close.

'Monsieur walks late,' said the first, a little confused, as it seemed, by that laugh.

'And will walk still later, if it pleases him,' said Roger. 'Good-night, my friends.'

'Ah!' said the second, 'friends do not say adieu so quickly. Monsieur will tell us the hour.'

'I have not a watch,' said Roger, quite truthfully.

'I will assist you to search for it,' said the third man, and laid a hand on his arm.

Roger threw it off. That was instinctive. One may be resigned to a man's knife between one's ribs, but not to his hands pawing one's shoulders. The man with the hand staggered back.

'The knife searches more surely,' said the second.

'No, no,' said the third quickly, 'he is too heavy. I for one will not carry him afterwards.'

They closed round him, hustling him between them. Their pale, degenerate faces spun and swung round him in the struggle. For there was a struggle. He had not meant that there should be a struggle. Someone would hear – someone would come.

But if any heard, none came. The street retained its empty silence, the houses, masked in close shutters, kept their reserve. The four were wrestling, all pressed close together in a writhing bunch, drawing breath hardly through set teeth, their feet slipping, and not slipping, on the rounded cobble-stones.

The contact with these creatures, the smell of them, the warm, greasy texture of their flesh as, in the conflict, his face or neck met neck or face of theirs   Roger felt a cold rage possess him. He wrung two clammy hands apart and threw something off – something that staggered back clattering, fell in the gutter, and lay there.

It was then that Roger felt the knife. Its point glanced off the cigarette-case in his breast pocket and bit sharply at his inner arm. And at the sting of it Roger knew that he did not desire to die. He feigned a reeling weakness, relaxed his grip, swayed sideways, and then suddenly caught the other two in a new grip, crushed their faces together, flung them off, and ran. It was but for an instant that his feet were the only ones that echoed in the street. Then he knew that the others too were running.

It was like one of those nightmares wherein one runs for ever, leaden-footed, through a city of the dead. Roger turned sharply to the right. The sound of the other footsteps told that the pursuers also had turned that corner. Here was another street – a steep ascent. He ran more swiftly – he was running now for his life – the life that he held so cheap three minutes before. And all the streets were empty – empty like dream-streets, with all their windows dark and unhelpful, their doors fast closed against his need.

Far away down the street and across steep roofs lay Paris, poured out like a pool of light in the mist of the valley. But Roger was running with his head down; he saw nothing but the round heads of the cobble stones. Only now and again he glanced to right or left, if perchance some window might show light to justify a cry for help, some door advance the welcome of an open inch.

There was at last such a door. He did not see it till it was almost behind him. Then there was the drag of the sudden stop – the eternal instant of indecision. Was there time? There must be. He dashed his fingers through the inch-crack, grazing the backs of them, leapt within, drew the door after him, felt madly for a lock or bolt, found a key, and, hanging his whole weight on it, strove to get the door home. The key turned. His left hand, by which he braced himself against the door-jamb, found a hook and pulled on it. Door and door-post met – the latch clicked – with a spring as it seemed. He turned the key, leaning against the door, which shook to the deep sobbing breaths that shook him, and to the panting bodies that pressed a moment without. Then someone cursed breathlessly outside; there was the sound of feet that went away.

Roger was alone in the strange darkness of an arched carriage-way, through the far end of which showed the fainter darkness of a courtyard, with black shapes of little formal tubbed orange trees. There was no sound at all there but the sound of his own desperate breathing; and, as he stood, the slow, warm blood crept down his wrist, to make a little pool in the hollow of his hanging, half-clenched hand. Suddenly he felt sick.

This house, of which he knew nothing, held for him no terrors. To him at that moment there were but three murderers in all the world, and where they were not, there safety was. But the spacious silence that soothed at first, presently clawed at the set, vibrating nerves already overstrained. He found himself listening, listening, and there was nothing to hear but the silence, and once, before he thought to twist his handkerchief round it, the drip of blood from his hand.

By and by, he knew that he was not alone in this house, for from far away there came the faint sound of a footstep, and, quite near, the faint answering echo of it. And at a window, high up on the other side of the courtyard, a light showed. Light and sound and echo intensified, the light passing window after window, till at last it moved across the courtyard, and the little trees threw back shifting shadows as it came towards him – a lamp in the hand of a man.

It was a short, bald man, with pointed beard and bright, friendly eyes. He held the lamp high as he came, and when he saw Roger, he drew his breath in an inspiration that spoke of surprise, sympathy, and pity.

'Hold! hold!' he said, in a singularly pleasant voice, 'there has been a misfortune? You are wounded, monsieur?'

'Apaches,' said Roger, and was surprised at the weakness of his own voice.

'Your hand?'

'My arm,' said Roger.

'Fortunately,' said the other, 'I am a surgeon. Allow me.'

He set the lamp on the step of a closed door, took off Roger's coat, and quickly tied his own handkerchief round the wounded arm.

'Now,' he said, 'courage! I am alone in the house. No one comes here but me. If you can walk up to my rooms, you will save us both much trouble. If you cannot, sit here and I will fetch you a cordial. But I advise you to try and walk. That *porte cochère* is, unfortunately, not very strong, and the lock is a common spring lock, and your friends may return with *their* friends; whereas the door across the courtyard is heavy and the bolts are new.'

Roger moved towards the heavy door whose bolts were new. The stairs seemed to go on for ever. The doctor lent his arm, but the carved bannisters and their lively shadows whirled before Roger's eyes. Also, he seemed to be shod with lead, and to have in his legs bones that were red-hot. Then the stairs ceased, and there was light, and a cessation of the dragging of those leaden feet. He was on a couch, and his eyes might close. There was no need to move any more, nor to look, nor to listen.

When next he saw and heard, he was lying at ease, the close intimacy of a bandage clasping his arm, and in his mouth the vivid taste of some cordial.

The doctor was sitting in an armchair near a table, looking benevolent through gold-rimmed pince-nez.

'Better?' he said. 'No, lie still, you'll be a new man soon.'

'I am desolated,' said Roger, 'to have occasioned you all this trouble.'

'Not at all,' said the doctor. 'We live to heal, and it is a nasty cut, that in your arm. If you are wise, you will rest at present. I shall be honoured if you will be my guest for the night.'

Roger again murmured something about trouble.

'In a big house like this,' said the doctor, as it seemed a little sadly, 'there are many empty rooms, and some rooms which are not empty. There is a bed altogether at your service, monsieur, and I counsel you not to delay in seeking it. You can walk?'

Wroxham stood up. 'Why, yes,' he said, stretching himself. 'I feel, as you say, a new man.'

A narrow bed and rush-bottomed chair showed like doll's-house furniture in the large, high, gaunt room to which the doctor led him.

'You are too tired to undress yourself,' said the doctor, 'rest - only rest,' and covered him with a rug, roundly tucked him up, and left him.

'I leave the door open,' he said, 'in case you have any fever. Good night. Do not torment yourself. All goes well.'

Then he took away the lamp, and Wroxham lay on his back and saw the shadows of the window-frames cast on the wall by the moon now risen. His eyes, growing accustomed to the darkness, perceived the carving of the white panelled walls and mantelpiece. There was a door in the room, another door from the one which the doctor had left open. Roger did not like open doors. The other door, however, was closed. He wondered where it led, and whether it was locked. Presently he got up to see. It was locked. He lay down again.

His arm gave him no pain, and the night's adventure did not seem to have overset his nerves. He felt, on the contrary, calm, confident, extraordinarily at ease, and master of himself. The trouble – how could that ever have seemed important? This calmness it felt like the calmness that precedes sleep. Yet sleep was far from him. What was it that kept sleep away? The bed was comfortable, the pillows soft. What was it? It came to him presently that it was the scent which distracted him, worrying him with a memory that he could not define. A faint scent of – what was it? Perfumery? Yes - and camphor - and something else - something vaguely disquieting. He had not noticed it before he had risen and tried the handle of that other door. But now ! . . He covered his face with the sheet, but through the sheet he smelt it still. He rose and threw back one of the long French windows. It opened with a click and a jar, and he looked across the dark well of the court-yard. He leaned out, breathing the chill, pure air of the May night, but when he withdrew his head, the scent was there again. Camphor - perfume - and something else. What was it that it reminded him of? He had his knee on the bed-edge when the answer came to that question. It was the scent that had struck at him from a darkened room when, a child, clutching at a grown-up hand, he had been led to the bed where, amid flowers, something white lay under a sheet – his mother, they had told him. It was the scent of death, disguised with drugs and perfumes.

He stood up and went, with carefully controlled swiftness, towards the open door. He wanted light and a human voice. The doctor was in the room upstairs; he ...

The doctor was face to face with him on the landing, not a yard away, moving towards him quietly in shoeless feet.

'I can't sleep,' said Wroxham, a little wildly, 'it's too dark – '

'Come upstairs,' said the doctor, and Wroxham went.

There was comfort in the large, lighted room, with its shelves and shelves full of well-bound books, its tables heaped with papers and pamphlets – its air of natural everyday work. There was a warmth of red curtain at the windows. On the window ledge a plant in a pot, its leaves like red misshapen hearts. A green-shaded lamp stood on the table. A peaceful, pleasant interior.

'What's behind that door,' said Wroxham, abruptly – 'that door downstairs?'

'Specimens,' the doctor answered, 'preserved specimens. My line is physiological research. You understand?'

So that was it.

'I feel quite well, you know,' said Wroxham, laboriously explaining – 'fit as any man – only I can't sleep.'

'I see,' said the doctor. .

'It's the scent from your specimens, I think,' Wroxham went on; 'there's something about that scent – '

'Yes,' said the doctor.

'It's very odd.' Wroxham was leaning his elbow on his knee and his chin on his hand. 'I feel so frightfully well – and yet – there's a strange feeling – '

'Yes,' said the doctor. 'Yes, tell me exactly what you feel.'

'I feel,' said Wroxham, slowly, 'like a man on the crest of a wave.'

The doctor stood up.

'You feel well, happy, full of life and energy – as though you could walk to the world's end, and yet . . .'

'And yet,' said Roger, 'as though my next step might be my last – as though I might step into my grave.'

He shuddered.

'Do you,' asked the doctor, anxiously – 'do you feel thrills of pleasure – something like the first waves of chloroform – thrills running from your hair to your feet?'

'I felt all that,' said Roger, slowly, 'downstairs before I opened the window.'

The doctor looked at his watch, frowned and got up quickly. 'There is very little time,' he said.

Suddenly Roger felt an unexplained opposition stiffen his mind.

The doctor went to a long laboratory bench with bottle-filled shelves above it, and on it crucibles and retorts, test tubes, beakers – all a chemist's apparatus – reached a bottle from a shelf, and measured out certain drops into a graduated glass, added water, and stirred it with a glass rod.

'Drink that,' he said.

'No,' said Roger, and as he spoke a thrill like the first thrill of the first chloroform wave swept through him, and it was a thrill, not of pleasure, but of pain. 'No,' he said, and 'Ah!' for the pain was sharp.

'If you don't drink,' said the doctor, carefully, 'you are a dead man.'

'You may be giving me poison,' Roger gasped, his hands at his heart.

'I may,' said the doctor. 'What do you suppose poison makes you feel like? What do you feel like now?'

'I feel,' said Roger, 'like death.'

Every nerve, every muscle thrilled to a pain not too intense to be underlined by a shuddering nausea.

'Then drink,' cried the doctor, in tones of such cordial entreaty, such evident anxiety, that Wroxham half held his hand out for the glass. 'Drink! Believe me, it is your only chance.'

Again the pain swept through him like an electric current. The beads of sweat sprang out on his forehead.

'That wound,' the doctor pleaded, standing over him with the glass held out. 'For God's sake, drink! Don't you understand, man? You *are* poisoned. Your wound ...'

'The knife?' Wroxham murmured, and as he spoke, his eyes seemed to swell in his head, and his head itself to grow enormous. 'Do you know the poison – and its antidote?'

'I know all.' The doctor soothed him. 'Drink, then, my friend.'

As the pain caught him again in a clasp more close than any lover's he clutched at the glass and drank. The drug met the pain and mastered it. Roger, in the ecstasy of pain's cessation, saw the world fade and go out in a haze of vivid violet.

II

Faint films of lassitude, shot with contentment, wrapped him round. He lay passive, as a man lies in the convalescence that follows a long fight with Death. Fold on fold of white peace lay all about him.

'I'm better now,' he said, in a voice that was a whisper – tried to raise his hand from where it lay helpless in his sight, failed, and lay looking at it in confident repose – 'much better.'

'Yes,' said the doctor, and his pleasant, soft voice had grown softer, pleasanter. 'You are now in the second stage. An interval is necessary before you can pass to the third. I will enliven the interval by conversation. Is there anything you would like to know?'

'Nothing,' said Roger; 'I am quite contented.'

'This is very interesting,' said the doctor. 'Tell me exactly how you feel.'

Roger faintly and slowly told him.

'Ah!' the doctor said, 'I have not before heard this. You are the only one of them all who ever passed the first stage. The others – '

'The others?' said Roger, but he did not care much about the others.

'The others,' said the doctor frowning, 'were unsound. Decadent students, degenerate, Apaches. You are highly trained – in fine physical condition. And your brain! God be good to the Apaches, who so delicately excited it to just the degree of activity needed for my purpose.'

'The others?' Wroxham insisted.

'The others? They are in the room whose door was locked. Look – you should be able to see them. The second drug should lay your consciousness before me, like a sheet of white paper on which I can write what I choose. If I choose that you should see my specimens – *Allons donc*. I have no secrets from you now. Look – look – strain your eyes. In theory, I know all that you can do and feel and see in this second stage. But practically – enlighten me – look – shut your eyes and look!'

Roger closed his eyes and looked. He saw the gaunt, uncarpeted staircase, the open doors of the big rooms, passed to the locked door, and it opened at his touch. The room inside was like the others, spacious and panelled. A lighted lamp with a blue shade hung from the ceiling, and below it an effect of spread whiteness. Roger looked. There *were* things to be seen.

With a shudder he opened his eyes on the doctor's delightful room, the doctor's intent face.

'What did you see?' the doctor asked. 'Tell me!'

'Did you kill them all?' Roger asked back.

'They died – of their own inherent weakness,' the doctor said. 'And you saw them?'

'I saw,' said Roger, 'the quiet people lying all along the floor in their death clothes – the people who have come in at that door of yours that is a trap – for robbery, or curiosity, or shelter, and never gone out any more.'

'Right,' said the doctor. 'Right. My theory is proved at every point. You can see what I choose you to see. Yes, decadents all. It was in embalming that I was a specialist before I began these other investigations.'

'What,' Roger whispered – 'what is it all for?'

'To make the superman,' said the doctor. 'I will tell you.'

He told. It was a long story – the story of a man's life, a man's work, a man's dreams, hopes, ambitions.

'The secret of life,' the doctor ended, 'that is what all the alchemists sought. They sought it where Fate pleased. I sought it where I have found it – in death.'

Roger thought of the room behind the locked door.

'And the secret is?' he asked.

'I have told you,' said the doctor impatiently; 'it is in the third drug that life – splendid, superhuman life – is found. I have tried it on animals. Always they became perfect, all that an animal should be. And more, too – much more. They were too perfect, too near humanity. They looked at me with human eyes. I could not let them live. Such animals it is not necessary to embalm. I had a laboratory in those days – and assistants. They called me the Prince of Vivisectors.'

The man on the sofa shuddered.

'I am naturally,' the doctor went on, 'a tender-hearted man. You see it in my face; my voice proclaims it. Think what I have suffered in the sufferings of these poor beasts who never injured me. My God! Bear witness that I have not buried my talent. I have been faithful. I have laid down all – love, and joy, and pity, and the little beautiful things of life – all, all, on the altar of science, and seen them consume away. I deserve my heaven, if ever man did. And now by all the saints in heaven I am near it!'

'What is the third drug?' Roger asked, lying limp and flat on his couch.

'It is the Elixir of Life,' said the doctor. 'I am not its discoverer; the old alchemists knew it well, but they failed because they sought to apply the elixir to a normal - that is, a diseased and faulty - body. I knew better. One must have first a body abnormally healthy, abnormally strong. Then, not the elixir, but the two drugs that prepare. The first excites prematurely the natural conflict between the principles of life and death, and then, just at the point where Death is about to win his victory, the second drug intensifies life so that it conquers - intensifies, and yet chastens. Then the whole life of the subject, risen to an ecstasy, falls prone in an almost voluntary submission to the coming super-life. Submission - submission! The garrison must surrender before the splendid conqueror can enter and make the citadel his own. Do you understand? Do you submit?'

'I submit,' said Roger, for, indeed, he did. 'But soon - quite soon - I will not submit.'

He was too weak to be wise, or those words had remained unspoken.

The doctor sprang to his feet.

'It works too quickly!' he cried. 'Everything works too quickly with you. Your condition is too perfect. So now I bind you.'

From a drawer beneath the bench where the bottles gleamed, the doctor drew rolls of bandages - violet, like the haze that had drowned, at the urgence of the second drug, the consciousness of Roger. He moved, faintly resistant, on his couch. The doctor's hands, most gently, most irresistibly, controlled his movement.

'Lie still,' said the gentle, charming voice. 'Lie still; all is well.' The clever, soft hands were unrolling the bandages - passing them round arms and throat - under and over the soft narrow couch. 'I cannot risk your life, my poor boy. The least movement of yours might ruin everything. The third drug, like the first, must be offered directly to the blood which absorbs it. I bound the first drug as an unguent upon your knife-wound.'

The swift hands, the soft bandages, passed back and

forth, over and under – flashes of violet passed to and fro in the air, like the shuttle of a weaver through his warp. As the bandage clasped his knees, Roger moved.

'For God's sake, no!' the doctor cried; 'the time is so near. If you cease to submit it is death.'

With an incredible, accelerated swiftness he swept the bandages round and round knees and ankles, drew a deep breath   stood upright. 'I must make an incision,' he said, 'in the head this time. It will not hurt. See! I spray it with the Constantia Nepenthe; that also I discovered. My boy, in a moment you know all things – you are as God. For God's sake, be patient. Preserve your submission.'

And Roger, with life and will resurgent hammering at his heart, preserved it.

He did not feel the knife that made the cross-cut on his temple, but he felt the hot spurt of blood that followed the cut; he felt the cool flap of a plaster, spread with some sweet, clean-smelling unguent that met the blood and staunched it. There was a moment – or was it hours? – of nothingness. Then from that cut on his forehead there seemed to radiate threads of infinite length, and of a strength that one could trust to – threads that linked one to all knowledge past and present. He felt that he controlled all wisdom, as a driver controls his four-in-hand. Knowledge, he perceived, belonged to him, as the air belongs to the eagle. He swam in it, as a great fish in a limitless ocean.

He opened his eyes and met those of the doctor, who sighed as one to whom breath has grown difficult.

'Ah, all goes well. Oh, my boy, was it not worth it? What do you feel?'

'I. Know. Everything,' said Roger, with full stops between the words.

'Everything? The future?'

'No. I know all that man has ever known.'

'Look back – into the past. See someone. See Pharaoh. You see him – on his throne?'

'Not on his throne. He is whispering in a corner of his great gardens to a girl, who is the daughter of a water-carrier.'

'Bah! Any poet of my dozen decadents, who lie so still could have told me that. Tell me secrets – the *Masque de Fer*.'

The other told a tale, wild and incredible, but it satisfied the teller.

'That too – it might be imagination. Tell me the name of the woman I loved and – '

The echo of the name of the anaesthetic came to Roger; 'Constantia,' said he, in an even voice.

'Ah,' the doctor cried, 'now I see you know all things. It was not murder. I hoped to dower her with all the splendours of the superlife.'

'Her bones lie under the lilacs, where you used to kiss her in the spring,' said Roger, quite without knowing what it was that he was going to say.

'It is enough,' the doctor cried. He sprang up, ranged certain bottles and glasses on a table convenient to his chair. 'You know all things. It was not a dream, this, the dream of my life. It is true. It is a fact accomplished. Now I, too, will know all things. I will be as the gods.'

He sought among leather cases on a far table, and came back swiftly into the circle of light that lay below the green-shaded lamp.

Roger, floating contentedly on the new sea of knowledge that seemed to support him, turned eyes on the trouble that had driven him out of that large, empty studio so long ago, so far away. His new-found wisdom laughed at that problem, laughed and solved it. 'To end that trouble I must do so-and-so, and say such-and-such,' Roger told himself again and again.

And now the doctor, standing by the table, laid on it his pale, plump hand outspread. He drew a knife from a case – a long, shiny knife – and scored his hand across and across its back, as a cook scores pork for cooking. The slow blood followed the cuts in beads and lines.

Into the cuts he dropped a green liquid from a little bottle, replaced its stopper, bound up his hand and sat down.

'The beginning of the first stage,' he said; 'almost at once I shall begin to be a new man. It will work quickly. My body, like yours, is sane and healthy.'

There was a long silence.

'Oh, but this is good,' the doctor broke it to say. 'I feel the hand of Life sweeping my nerves like harp-strings.'

Roger had been thinking, the old common sense that guides an ordinary man breaking through this consciousness of illimitable wisdom. 'You had better,' he said, 'unbind me; when the hand of Death sweeps your nerves, you may need help.'

'No,' the doctor said, 'and no, and no, and no many times. I am afraid of you. You know all things, and even in your body you are stronger than I. When I, too, am a god, and filled with the wine of knowledge, I will loose you, and together we will drink of the fourth drug – the mordant that shall fix the others and set us eternally on a level with the immortals.'

'Just as you like, of course,' said Roger, with a conscious effort after commonplace. Then suddenly, not commonplace any more –

'Loose me!' he cried; 'loose me, I tell you! I am wiser than you.'

'You are also stronger,' said the doctor, and then suddenly and irresistibly the pain caught him. Roger saw his face contorted with agony, his hands clench on the arm of his chair; and it seemed that, either this man was less able to bear pain than he, or that the pain was much more violent than had been his own. Between the grippings of the anguish the doctor dragged on his watch-chain; the watch leapt from his pocket, and rattled as his trembling hand laid it on the table.

'Not yet,' he said, when he had looked at its face, 'not

yet, not yet, not yet.' It seemed to Roger, lying there bound, that the other man repeated those words for long days and weeks. And the plump, pale hand, writhing and distorted by anguish, again and again drew near to take the glass that stood ready on the table, and with convulsive self-restraint again and again drew back without it.

The short May night was waning – the shiver of dawn rustled the leaves of the plant whose leaves were like red misshaped hearts.

'Now!' The doctor screamed the word, grasped the glass, drained it and sank back in his chair. His hand struck the table beside him. Looking at his limp body and head thrown back, one could almost see the cessation of pain, the coming of kind oblivion.

III

The dawn had grown to daylight, a poor, grey, rain-stained daylight, not strong enough to pierce the curtains and persiennes, and yet not so weak but that it could mock the lamp, now burnt low and smelling vilely.

Roger lay very still on his couch, a man wounded, anxious, and extravagantly tired. In those hours of long, slow dawning, face to face with the unconscious figure in the chair, he had felt, slowly and little by little, the recession of that sea of knowledge on which he had felt himself float in such content. The sea had withdrawn itself, leaving him high and dry on the shore of the normal. The only relic that he had clung to and that he still grasped was the answer to the problem of the trouble – the only wisdom that he had put into words. These words remained to him, and he knew that they held wisdom – very simple wisdom, too.

'To end the trouble, I must do so-and-so and say such-and-such.'

But of all that had seemed to set him on a pinnacle, had evened him with the immortals, nothing else was left. He was just Roger Wroxham – wounded, and bound, in a locked house, one of whose rooms was full of very quiet people, and in another room himself and a dead man. For now it was so long since the doctor had moved that it seemed he must be dead. He had got to know every line of that room, every fold of drapery, every flower on the wall-paper, the number of the books, the shapes and sizes of things. Now he could no longer look at these. He looked at the other man.

Slowly a dampness spread itself over Wroxham's forehead and tingled among the roots of his hair. He writhed in his bonds. They held fast. He could not move hand or foot. Only his head could turn a little, so that he could at will see the doctor or not see him. A shaft of desolate light pierced the persienne at its hinge and rested on the table, where an overturned glass lay.

Wroxham thrilled from head to foot. The body in the chair stirred – hardly stirred – shivered rather – and a very faint, far-away voice said:–

'Now the third – give me the third.'

'What?' said Roger, stupidly; and he had to clear his throat twice before he could say even that.

'The moment is now,' said the doctor. 'I remember all. I made you a god. Give me the third drug.'

'Where is it?' Roger asked.

'It is at my elbow,' the doctor murmured. 'I submit – I submit. Give me the third drug, and let me be as you are.'

'As *I* am?' said Roger. 'You forget. *I* am bound.'

'Break your bonds,' the doctor urged, in a quick, small voice. 'I trust you now. You are stronger than all men, as you are wiser. Stretch your muscles, and the bandages will fall asunder like snow-wreaths.'

'It is too late,' Wroxham said, and laughed; 'all that is over. I am not wise any more, and I have only the strength of a man. I am tired and wounded. I cannot break your bonds – I cannot help you!'

'But if you cannot help me – it is death,' said the doctor.

'It is death,' said Roger. 'Do you feel it coming on you?'

'I feel life returning,' said the doctor; 'it is now the moment – the one possible moment. And I cannot reach it. Oh, give it me – give it me!'

Then Roger cried out suddenly, in a loud voice: 'Now, by God in heaven, you damned decadent, I am *glad* that I cannot give it. Yes if it costs me my life, it's worth it, you madman, so that your life ends too. Now be silent, and die like a man, if you have it in you.'

Only one word seemed to reach the man in the chair.

'A decadent!' he repeated. 'I? But no, I am like you – I see what I will. I close my eyes, and I see – no – not that – ah! not that!' He writhed faintly in his chair, and to Roger it seemed that for that writhing figure there would be no return of power and life and will.

'Not that,' he moaned. 'Not that,' and writhed in a gasping anguish that bore no more words.

Roger lay and watched him, and presently he writhed from the chair to the floor, tearing feebly at it with his fingers, moaned, shuddered, and lay very still.

Of all that befell Roger in that house, the worst was now. For now he knew that he was alone with the dead, and between him and death stretched certain hours and days. For the *porte cochère* was locked; the doors of the house itself were locked – heavy doors and the locks new.

'I am alone in the house,' the doctor had said. 'No one comes here but me.'

No one would come. He would die there – he, Roger Wroxham – 'poor old Roger Wroxham, who was no one's enemy but his own.' Tears pricked his eyes. He shook his head impatiently and they fell from his lashes.

'You fool,' he said, 'can't *you* die like a man either?'

Then he set his teeth and made himself lie still. It seemed to him that now Despair laid her hand on his heart. But, to speak truth, it was Hope whose hand lay there. This was so much more than a man should be called on to bear – it could not be true. It was an evil dream. He would wake presently. Or if it were, indeed, real – then someone would come, someone must come. God could not let nobody come to save him.

And late at night, when heart and brain had been stretched to the point where both break and let in the sea of madness, someone came.

The interminable day had worn itself out. Roger had screamed, yelled, shouted till his throat was dried up, his lips baked and cracked. No one heard. How should they? The twilight had thickened and thickened, till at last it made a shroud for the dead man on the floor by the chair. And there were other dead men in that house; and as Roger ceased to see the one he saw the others – the quiet, awful faces, the lean hands, the straight, stiff limbs laid out one beyond another in the room of death. They at least were not bound. If they should rise in their white wrappings and, crossing that empty sleeping chamber very softly, come slowly up the stairs –

A stair creaked.

His ears, strained with hours of listening, thought themselves befooled. But his cowering heart knew better.

Again a stair creaked. There was a hand on the door.

'Then it is all over,' said Roger in the darkness, 'and I *am* mad.'

The door opened very slowly, very cautiously. There was no light. Only the sound of soft feet and draperies that rustled.

Then suddenly a match spurted – light struck at his eyes; a flicker of lit candle-wick steadying to flame. And the things that had come were not those quiet people creeping up to match their death with his death in life, but human creatures, alive, breathing, with eyes that moved and glittered, lips that breathed and spoke.

'He must be here,' one said. 'Lisette watched all day; he never came out. He must be here – there is nowhere else.'

Then they set up the candle-end on the table, and he saw their faces. They were the Apaches who had set on

him in that lonely street, and who had sought him here –
to set on him again.

He sucked his dry tongue, licked his dry lips, and cried
aloud:–

'Here I am! Oh, kill me! For the love of God, brothers,
kill me *now*!'

And even before he spoke, they had seen him, and seen
what lay on the floor.

'He died this morning. I am bound. Kill me, brothers;
I cannot die slowly here alone. Oh, kill me, for Christ's
sake!'

But already the three were pressing on each other at a
doorway suddenly grown too narrow. They could kill a
living man, but they could not face death, quiet, en-
throned.

'For the love of Christ,' Roger screamed, 'have pity! Kill
me outright! Come back – come back!'

And then, since even Apaches are human, one of them
did come back. It was the one he had flung into the gutter.
The feet of the others sounded on the stairs as he caught
up the candle and bent over Roger, knife in hand.

'Make sure,' said Roger, through set teeth.

'*Nom d'un nom*,' said the Apache, with worse words, and
cut the bandages here, and here, and here again, and
there, and lower, to the very feet.

Then this good Samaritan helped Roger to rise, and
when he could not stand, the Samaritan half pulled, half
carried him down those many steps, till they came upon
the others putting on their boots at the stair-foot.

Then between them the three men who could walk
carried the other out and slammed the outer door, and
presently set him against a gate-post in another street, and
went their wicked ways.

And after a time, a girl with furtive eyes brought brandy
and hoarse, muttered kindnesses, and slid away in the
shadows.

Against that gate-post the police came upon him. They

took him to the address they found on him. When they came to question him he said, 'Apaches,' and his late variations on that theme were deemed sufficient, though not one of them touched truth or spoke of the third drug.

There has never been anything in the papers about that house. I think it is still closed, and inside it still lie in the locked room the very quiet people; and above, there is the room with the narrow couch and the scattered, cut, violet bandages, and the thing on the floor by the chair, under the lamp that burned itself out in that May dawning.